DEKOK AND
MURDER IN SEANCE

"DeKok" Books by A.C. Baantjer:

Published in the United States:

Murder in Amsterdam
DeKok and the Sunday Strangler
DeKok and the Corpse on Christmas Eve
DeKok and the Somber Nude
DeKok and the Dead Harlequin
DeKok and the Sorrowing Tomcat
DeKok and the Disillusioned Corpse
DeKok and the Careful Killer
DeKok and the Romantic Murder
DeKok and the Dying Stroller
DeKok and the Corpse at the Church Wall
DeKok and the Dancing Death
DeKok and the Naked Lady
DeKok and the Brothers of the Easy Death
DeKok and the Deadly Accord
DeKok and Murder in Seance
DeKok and Murder on the Menu

Available soon from InterContinental Publishing:

DeKok and Murder in Ecstasy
DeKok and the Begging Death
DeKok and the Geese of Death
DeKok and Murder by Melody
DeKok and Death of a Clown
DeKok and Variations on Murder
DeKok and Murder by Installments
DeKok and Murder on Blood Mountain
DeKok and the Dead Lovers
DeKok and the Mask of Death
DeKok and the Corpse by Return
DeKok and Murder in Bronze
DeKok and the Deadly Warning
DeKok and Murder First Class
DeKok and the Vendetta
DeKok and Murder Depicted
DeKok and Dance Macabre
DeKok and the Disfiguring Death
DeKok and the Devil's Conspiracy
DeKok and the Duel at Night
and more . . .

DeKok and Murder in Seance

by

BAANTJER

translated from the Dutch by H.G. Smittenaar

INTERCONTINENTAL PUBLISHING

ISBN 1 881164 15 2

Printing History:

1st Dutch printing: 1981
16th Dutch printing: 1996

1st American edition: 1996

Typography: Monica S. Rozier
Cover Design: InterContinental Publishing

Cover Photo: Studio Myosotis (Netherlands)

Library of Congress Cataloging-in-Publication Data

Baantjer, A. C.
[De Cock en de moord in seance. English]
DeKok and murder in seance / by Baantjer ; translated from the Dutch by H.G. Smittenaar.
p. cm
ISBN 1–881164–15–2
I. Smittenaar, H. G. II. Title.
PT5881. 12.A2C56513 1996
839.3'1364—dc21 96–48758
CIP

DeKok
and
Murder in Seance

1

Jennifer Jordan rubbed her clammy, perspiring forehead with the back of her hand. She was confused, unsure of herself. It was an uncomfortable feeling for which she could find no reasonable explanation. With her sharp hearing she tried to analyze the sounds in the room. The shuffling of feet across the Berber carpet, the mumbling of a whispered conversation near the window, the rattling of the porcelain cup diagonally across from her on the large, round oaken table.

She knew exactly which women were present. She knew them all by their names, the sound of their voices, the rustling of their clothes and the subtle aroma of their perfumes. Only with Christine, her faithful friend, did she keep closer relations. The others she knew but superficially from the weekly seances in her house. She had never seen the young ones at all. She remembered the faces of the older ones.

She wondered how the faces in her memory had been changed. How had the lines formed, the creases deepened? Had the faces become sharper? Like her own? When she stroked her sensitive fingertips over her own face, she discovered wrinkles around her eyes, deep creases around her mouth and other blemishes on her once so smooth skin.

As usual, while preparing herself mentally, she drifted into reminisences. And, also as usual, she returned to one of the most important, decisive days in her life. Seventeen years ago it had started. She remembered the moment exactly, like a bright photograph. It had been a sunny morning in May. The rattling of the alarm clock on the walnut bedside table had torn her away from a sweet slumber. Then she had opened her eyes to stare at the ceiling for several minutes. She did that every morning. She would stare at the ceiling and listen to the early sounds of the canal outside her bedroom window. That day the sounds had been there, intense, sharper than ever. But the play of white and dark from the ceiling, supported by oak beams, had been missing. It remained dark. It remained night. An impenetrable darkness. At first she had been surprised. How was that possible? Then came fear, followed by panic. She knew it was daylight because from her left, through the window, she could feel the heat of the morning sun on her skin. Slowly, very slowly came the realization, she acknowledged the reality. The opening and closing of her eyelids had no effect. There was no change from dark to light. She could not see any more. She was blind.

She felt for the arm of Christine, her friend.

"Are they all here?"

Christine leaned closer.

"Black Julie isn't here yet," she whispered. "It's the same every time. She's always late. We should start without her, that would teach her a lesson."

Jennifer smiled indulgently.

"We better wait for her. I like having her in the circle. She's so stimulating. I always have good contacts when she's part of it. Last week I was convinced that the astral body of great-aunt Emelia was present."

Christine nodded, but Jennifer did not see it.

"It was an exquisite seance," she said decorously. "very beautiful. I hope that tonight, too, the spirits are willing. The signs are felicitous. Perhaps even a real materialization."

Jennifer Jordan lowered her head to the table.

"That hasn't happened in years," she said dully.

Christine laughed.

"Not so somber. You're a fantastic medium. Everybody knows that. Even Professor Havelte has lauded you most eloquently." Christine pressed the back of her hand to Jennifer's cheek. "How are you feeling today?" There was concern in her voice.

Jennifer did not answer. Again her thoughts went back to the past. She had never accepted that terrible realization. She had never resigned herself to her blindness. She was just a little less desperate than in the past. The years had taught her to live with her blindness, to exist in the dark. But in her heart she nurtured the inner certainty that one day, some day, she would see again. That certainty, that inner awareness had given her the courage to persevere, despite many disappointments. She had had her eyes examined scores of times. And time and again she had been assured that medical science had not progressed to the point where it could help her. But the latest specialist, whom she had visited on the urging of some far-away acquaintances, had given her new hope. He was willing to try, he had said. It would be a dangerous operation, a bold gamble to re-open her eyes to the ever changing interplay of light and colors. It was strange that the idea scared her. Her initial happiness was overshadowed by an increasing fear, as if she was afraid of a truth, a new truth that was present, but she could not see. Not now.

* * *

She felt Christine touching her arm.

"Black Julie is here." There was an undertone of irritation. "She just came in. When madam has taken off her coat, we can finally start. The others are getting impatient." She paused. "You should talk to her about it."

Jennifer Jordan nodded resignedly.

"Put Julie on my left at the table. That's were she was last week as well. There was a real supporting power coming from her."

She sensed the irritation in the way Christine moved.

"As you will," said Christine, capitulating. "That spot is still empty. Well, what do you think? You want to start with the Ouija board?"

Jennifer sat up straight and pushed her hands out of the wide sleeves of the shiny black toga she wore.

"All right, Christine. That's a good idea." She felt Black Julie fall in the chair next to her. The woman was breathing hard. She waited until she heard the breathing become more regular. "Are we all seated?" she asked.

There was an consenting murmur from around the table.

"Are the curtains closed tight? Is the light dimmed?"

"Everything and everybody is ready," said Christine.

"When do you serve the coffee?"

"After the Ouija board. They all had coffee when they came in and Harry has taken the dishes away. He'll wash them and bring them back later. He's also taken care of the music."

Jennifer Jordan nodded her agreement with the arrangements. She made her face expressionless and stood up. She looked impressive, almost sinister. The pale color of her face and hands contrasted sharply with the black toga. The blind eyes stared at nothing.

"Does anybody in the circle have an important announcement? If so, speak now."

There was the rustle of a silk dress from the opposite side of the table. Agatha Cologne stood up. She folded her hands devoutly in front of her chest. There was a sorrowing look on her wrinkled face.

"My sister Martha," she said softly, "passed away peacefully last Tuesday." She paused and waited for the hasty whispers to cease. "Martha was tired and her old heart had nothing left to give. The time was too short to let you all know personally. I've only been able to inform a few of you. As soon as possible I will talk to you all individually." She looked around, unclasped her hands. "It is my request that our medium try to establish contact with Martha. I would dearly love to know how it is with her."

Jennifer Jordan coughed discreetly.

"I have heard about Martha's death. Our sincere condolences. I'm sure that the passing of our dear friend Martha has touched all of us deeply and the thought of her death makes all of us feel sad." She paused while her blind eyes went around the table. Then she changed her tone of voice. "However, it is not my habit to call on the spirits of the dear departed this soon after they have passed on. We must give them time to adapt to their new environment."

Agatha's reaction was unusually sharp.

"I asked Martha." Her high, shrill voice became more shrill. "I held her hand during the last moments and asked her if we could call on her during the next seance." She swallowed. "My sister was extremely clear of mind, just before she died. She was happy and gave me an encouraging nod. 'Ask Jennifer,' she said."

Christine came to her blind friend's aid.

"If Jennifer says," she said unctuously, "that we should not disturb the spirits of the recently departed, then we should respect that opinion. Jennifer is more familiar with the spirit world than we. Please keep in mind that it is only through *her* that we can make contact with the realm of the shades."

Black Julie stood up.

"I think Jennifer should try. If Martha promised her sister that she would manifest herself to us after her death, then Martha will do so. She owes Agatha a lot. Agatha has taken care of Martha all her life."

Jennifer pressed her lips together, a determined look on her face.

"In the world of the spirits," she said pointedly, "there are different rules from those here on earth."

Agatha Cologne waved her short arms.

"Martha always loved us," she cried out. "Her spirit will do the same."

Diagonally across from Christine, Annette Leeuwenhoek suddenly came to her feet. She wiped the long gray hair from her face.

"What does such a promise mean," she protested emotionally. "What does it mean when Martha promises to visit us after her death? We all knew Martha. We all know how she was. She has often said things, declared things, that were, to say the least, open to interpretation."

Little Agatha snorted angrily. She leaned forward, her hands on the table. Her dark-brown eyes flickered evilly.

"You're not saying," she blustered, "that Martha *lied* in her dying hour!?"

Annette did not answer. She turned away from Agatha and pointed a finger at Black Julie.

"A few days before her death, Martha came to visit me. At home. Just to gossip about you. She said the most terrible things . . . I won't dignify it by repeating her accusations. But if Martha *dares* to manifest herself here as a spirit, I *do* want to ask her for clarification about a number of things." Her tone was mocking and challenging.

Agatha Cologne was boiling mad. Her face was red and her hands looked like claws.

"Martha could say a thing or two about *you*," she snarled. She addressed the table. "Just ask her how her first husband died."

Black Julie looked at Annette, fear in her eyes.

"What did Martha say about me?" she asked tonelessly.

Jennifer Jordan raised her arms in a gesture of supplication.

"Let us leave this subject until *after* the coffee," she said, a cynical tone in her voice. "I propose that then we can vote on whether or not to call upon the spirit of Martha Cologne. Although I personally object, I will obey the rule of the majority ... but I warn you: as I listen to you, I'm afraid there might be consequences."

She sighed deeply and felt for the cross in the hoop on the table. Lightly she took it in her hand. She felt the shape of the object. A simple cross, nailed inside a hoop of light wood. At the intersection of the two cross-pieces, a pointer descended. One or more people would lightly support the encircling hoop and hopefully the object would be moved by the spirits so that the pointer would point at different letters, or numbers. In her mind's eye she saw the board with its letters and numbers, the words *yes* and *no*. She had expected a lot from this session. The results of last week seemed to justify that. She had prepared well, but a common quarrel between members of the circle had disturbed her concentration. She felt the relaxed mood disappear, the mood that was so essential for a good medium. The world of the spirits seemed far away, the shades unreachable. And yet she felt tension in her immediate environment, the vibrations of lusts, strong emotions. Something was happening around her ... something dramatic ... lugubrious ... something she could not control. For a few seconds she wished fervently for the ability to see . . . to see the faces around her . . . the eyes, the mouths, the expressions of hate, envy and . . . murder.

"Pick up the cross," she ordered. Her voice was harder than she meant it to be. "Open yourselves to receive the spirits." She felt how the hands of the others supported the instrument. It moved slightly as each of them found the most comfortable way to support the negligible weight. She felt the pointer move, aimlessly at first, then more positively. She tried to guide it, but was unable to do so. A force stronger than her, stronger than any of the others, had taken control.

"J," whispered Christine next to her. "A, N and an E." Christine's voice hesitated. "The call is for Jane." An oppressive silence fell over them, almost tangible. "Who is Jane?"

Nobody in the circle answered.

"Who is Jane," repeated Christine hoarsely.

The silence cloaked them like a blanket. Then the cross moved again.

"D," whispered Christine. "Now an I, E and an S."

Jennifer heard Christine swallow. Then she found her voice.

"Jane dies," she laughed nervously. "That's the message: 'Jane dies.'"

With difficulty Jennifer pulled her hand from underneath the cross. She put her hands to her ears.

"Stop," she screamed. Sweat beaded her forehead. "Stop, there's an angry spirit among us . . . an evil spirit." She waved her arms around her. "Chase her away. Quick. Turn on the lights . . . open the curtains . . . chase her away."

Harry Donkers came running from the kitchen, a shocked look on his face. The lights came on. Nobody said a word. Nobody moved. They looked at each other with amazement and fear in their eyes. It took several minutes, several long minutes.

Then Jennifer sat back in her chair. The voices broke the silence and Christine signaled for coffee.

The strange happenings during the aborted seance kept all of them under a spell. But slowly they became more self-confident, less grave. They asked each other for whom the message could have been meant.

Suddenly Black Julie gripped her throat. Her face swelled, red, repulsive. Her eyes bulged, seemed to come out of their sockets. Then she slid on the floor.

Harry Donkers hastened forward and leaned over her. When he straightened out, he seemed dazed.

"Julie," he said slowly, "Julie is dead."

2

The decrepit police VW Beetle was parked between the trees along the side of the canal. Detective-Inspector DeKok of Warmoes Street station hoisted himself out of the car. He looked up at the 17th Century facades of the houses and turned to his partner, assistant and friend, Dick Vledder.

"Is this the address?"

"Yes," said Vledder, locking the car. "I don't know why I lock it," grumbled the young man, "you realize we're probably the only team still driving this old model car?"

"Perhaps because they're afraid I might drive it sometimes," joked DeKok. "What number?" he then asked businesslike.

"Number thirteen," answered Vledder.

They crossed the street which was actually a quay. The roads on either side of Amsterdam's canals were proper quays, but a real Amsterdammer refers to them as streets. The ubiquitous canals were so much a part of Amsterdam that the natives hardly remarked upon them.

They approached the typical canal house. Three to four stories high with an attic floor. The lower floor was built only halfway in the ground, separate stairs led down to the entrance of what used to be the servants quarters. Other, more ornate stairs led to the front door, half a floor up. The front door was not exactly in the center of the house to allow space for the block and tackle arrangement that protruded from the attic floor. When these houses were originally built, barges and ships would tie up in the canal across from the house. The merchant would have his goods hauled up to the attic floor for storage. Typically a merchant would live on the other floors with his family. Most houses actually leaned forward, were built that way, to facilitate the hoisting of goods and to protect them from banging against the walls of the house.

They climbed the bluestone steps to the front door. The heavy door was ajar. DeKok pushed it open. Through a spacious, marble foyer, they reached a wooden staircase. DeKok heaved his two hundred pounds up the narrow, steep staircase. Vledder followed close behind.

Harry Donkers was waiting for them on the second floor landing.

"Police?" he asked.

The gray sleuth smiled benignly.

"DeKok," he said, "with kay-oh-kay." He pointed behind him. "Vledder, my colleague."

Harry Donkers gestured nervously.

"She's in the living room," he swallowed. "On the carpet. As instructed, we didn't touch a thing. She's still in the same position. Dead. Murdered, we think, by a spirit."

DeKok was amazed.

"By a spirit, you say?" he asked. When he saw the man nod, he added: "You don't say."

"Oh, yes." said Donkers.

"What sort of spirit?"

Donkers hesitated.

"The spirit of a departed soul. She manifested herself during the seance."

DeKok snorted.

"Dead people are in Heaven, or in Hell," he said brusquely, "and I've never seen a murderer come from either place."

Vledder looked at his partner.

"I've heard you say that before."

"No doubt," answered DeKok. "And you might hear me say it again. It's the truth and I mean every word of it."

Harry Donkers led the way. At the end of the corridor he opened the door to a low, cozy room, supported by broad beams along the ceiling. That used to be necessary to support the weight of the spices, or whatever, on the upper floors, thought Vledder.

A group of women had gathered at the end of the room, near three narrow windows. Their nervous, anxious whispers stopped when the two Police Inspectors entered the room.

DeKok let his eyes roam around the room. The room was tastefully furnished. On the walls to left and right he discovered paintings by French impressionists: Renoir, Monet, Toulouse-Lautrec, painters he had admired for years.

In the center of the room was a large, round oaken table, surrounded by magnificent oak chairs with high backs. There were nine chairs. Only one was occupied.

A woman was seated in the chair. Silently, with folded hands in front of her on the table, dressed in a shiny black toga, she seemed to stare into the distance, not acknowledging the cops with so much as a flicker of her eyes. The chair next to her was pushed back. Next to that chair was the body of a woman, on her back, the legs, bent at the knees, slightly spread. The face was rigid, the gray-green eyes were frozen in a blind stare.

DeKok noted everything carefully. Not a single detail, no matter how small, escaped his searching eyes. It was almost as if a tape recorder went on in his head, years later he would still be able to remember the exact details. Vledder had once, jokingly, referred to DeKok's almost total re-call in terms of a video tape recorder. DeKok had been horrified. He abhorred all things modern.

DeKok approached the dead woman and kneeled down beside her. She was dead, there was no doubt about it. The heavy make-up on her face could not mask the color of death. He looked at the eyes. They were round, protruding and the pupils were clearly dilated. Again he looked at the face. She was no longer young. About forty, he thought, maybe older. The hair, probably gray, had been tinted black. It contrasted starkly with the white Berber carpet. There was no sign of a struggle on her clothes. The skirt was colorful and of a type that had recently been recalled because of its flammability. The heliotrope blouse was ruffled at the neck and wrist. The total impression was respectable, with just a hint of frivolity. He looked at the neck, but saw no sign of violence. He was just about to get up when he noticed a small stain on the front of the blouse, almost hidden by the wide collar. It was brown and irregularly shaped, as if she had spilled something.

Vledder came nearer.

"Has she been murdered?"

DeKok placed a hand on the oaken table and came up from the floor.

"The pupils are strongly dilated," he pointed out. "Very strongly dilated. I'm thinking in terms of *psychoanalecticum stimulantia*."

"What?"

DeKok suppressed a chuckle. He liked pulling Vledder's leg from time to time.

"A mind-bending, stimulating substance, such as *pervitine*, *scopolamine*, or cocaine."

"Doesn't have to be fatal, does it?"

"Not quickly, anyway. Of course, in the long run they will all kill you. No . . . I think it has been used in combination with something else."

"A strong poison?"

DeKok nodded slowly.

"Possibly. Some combinations make the poison act faster. We'll have to ask Dr. Eskes about that. Perhaps he knows about some examples."

"You're mistaken." She sounded sharp, chastising. "The spirits don't need poison when, in their wrath, they have damned an earthling."

DeKok looked into the blind eyes of the woman in the black toga.

"Was she damned?"

She nodded vehemently.

"It was her own fault. Black Julie was always late for the seances. The spirits took offense, that's quite clear, now."

DeKok's eyebrows vibrated. Unfortunately the blind woman was unable to see the spectacular sight. DeKok's eyebrows sometimes seemed to live a life of their own and in their occasional behavior resembled more the antennae of an insect than a part of human anatomy. At times the eyebrows seemed to literally dance of their own volition.

"You mean . . ." he prompted.

A woman left the group by the windows.

"This is Jennifer Jordan," she said hastily. "Our medium. She's blind."

Jennifer's mouth momentarily formed a hard line.

"The man can see that for himself, Christine," she chided. "It doesn't take a Police-Inspector to figure that out. Besides, I'm not here as an eyewitness."

DeKok could not suppress a smile.

"You're Christine?" he asked in a friendly tone of voice.

The woman stepped forward.

"Christine Vanwal. I'm a friend and sometimes the nurse for Jennifer. We live here together."

"And the young man who met us?"

She smiled.

"That's our Harry . . . Harry Donkers. Jennifer's nephew. The only son of her dead sister. He lives here too, sometimes. When amorous adventures do not require his presence elsewhere."

Jennifer was not amused.

"His private life is none of your business."

Christine tossed her head back.

"Did I lie?"

DeKok listened to the tone as much as to the content of the words. Something bothered him. He cocked his head and studied the woman intently, shamelessly, the way only a cop can look at a person, as if the person is no more than an object to be studied. He estimated her to be in her late forties. The black, graying hair had been combed back tightly and ended in a chignon. The oval, handsome face radiated with friendly congeniality. The whole countenance appeared amicable. Unfortunately, the effect was spoiled by the clear, green eyes. The eyes were cold, distant, passionless as the eyes of a snake.

"Can you tell us what happened this morning?"

She nodded slowly, as if gathering her thoughts.

"We held a seance," she began. "We do that every week, Thursdays. Our Jennifer is an excellent medium and she maintains good relationships with the realm of the shades. Although there are spiritualist groups who condemn our mind-set, we obtain remarkable results. During our last seance we even observed the manifestation of an astral body. Our expectations for today were heightened by it."

DeKok pointed at the high-backed chairs.

"Are the same people always part of the circle?"

Christine Vanwal turned around and pointed at the group of women.

"We've been getting together for years. There have been a few changes, but most of us already participated when Jennifer could still see. Isn't that right, Jennifer?"

Jennifer Jordan nodded. Her face was serious.

"We lost Martha Cologne last week. Rather sudden, I must say. She was spiritually very active. I really had not expected it so quickly. Last week she was still in our midst and now she's gone. Her sister, Agatha, wanted me to call on the spirit of Martha. I was against it, but Agatha and Black Julie urged me to do it."

DeKok rubbed the bridge of his nose with a little finger.

"And?" he asked, hesitating, "did Martha's spirit . . . eh, . . . manifest itself?"

Jennifer shrugged her shoulders in a helpless gesture.

"I never called on her. There was a disagreement and we decided to wait until we could vote on the subject . . . after the coffee." She sighed deeply. "We never reached that point, either. She would not allow it. The evil spirit struck before we could vote."

DeKok swallowed.

"Martha?"

There was a sorrowful look on Jennifer's face.

"I don't know."

"An evil spirit?"

She nodded impassionately.

"I clearly felt her presence. Almost right from the start of the seance, with the Ouija board. She almost seemed materialized . . . almost tangible." She sighed again, very deeply. Her body shook. "I immediately dropped the cross after the announcement and terminated the seance. The pressure on me was too heavy, too suffocating. I could not bear it any longer. That's when I realized the catastrophe could not be diverted."

"You could not prevent it?"

Jennifer spread her hands in a gesture of surrender.

"Who can stand against the will of an evil spirit?"

DeKok closed his eyes momentarily. The conversation tired him.

"What was that announcement?"

Jennifer Jordan stretched out a shaking hand toward the center of the table.

"The announcement appeared on the board. Christine read the letters out loud as the cross indicated them. They spelled the words 'Jane dies.' That was all."

"Who is Jane?"

Christine Vanwal shrugged her shoulders.

"I asked the same question myself, but nobody in the circle reacted. I don't know any Jane among us, either."

DeKok lightly touched the black toga.

"The announcement came from the evil spirit?"

Jennifer nodded.

"Absolutely . . . no doubt about it."

"And was meant for one of those present?"

The medium hesitated.

"That . . . that is . . . is usually the case," she stammered.

DeKok leaned closer. His face was expressionless.

"And nobody knows *Jane,* but Black Julie died."

An oppressive silence suddenly filled the room.

DeKok stood up straight and looked around. One of the women from near the windows came closer. She stopped in front of him and wiped the gray hair from her face.

"I'm Annette," she said formally. "Annette Leeuwenhoek. I have attended this seance and I can say truthfully that the prophecy has come true . . . *Jane died*!" She paused and with a dramatic gesture she pointed at the dead woman on the carpet. "Jane Truffle . . . once my brother's wife."

3

Dr. Koning, the old, small, always somewhat eccentric Municipal Coroner, entered the room with short, angry steps. Behind him towered two morgue attendants, a stretcher between them.

DeKok walked toward the Coroner. With a friendly smile he extended his hand.

"Sorry to bother you, doctor," he said apologetically, "but I've another one."

"What?"

DeKok spread his arms.

"A dead corpse."

Dr. Koning looked at him from over his half-glasses, a reproving look in his eyes.

"My friend," he said severely, "corpses are always dead. Just in case you did not know, being dead is the very essence of a corpse."

DeKok suppressed a smile. He knew the old doctor was completely serious. He bowed formally, as if accepting the rebuke, and led the doctor to the corpse. Weelen, the police photographer who had arrived just before the old man, was putting the finishing touches to his equipment. He gave DeKok a questioning look. DeKok held up his hand, indicating the photographer should wait. Together they watched the old doctor.

Doctor Koning took off his old, greenish Garibaldi hat, hitched up the trousers of his formal, striped pants and kneeled down. He lifted the dead woman's chin and peered intently at the neck. The tips of his fingers felt the back of her head. Then he took out a small flashlight and shined it into the eyes. After a long time, he hoisted himself to his feet. DeKok hastened to help the old man. There was a worried look on the Coroner's face.

"The woman is dead," he said softly.

"Thank you doctor," said DeKok formally. Under Dutch law the woman was now officially dead. "But," continued DeKok, "isn't it a bit strange that she still looks so healthy?"

"You mean the color of the face?"

"Indeed."

Doctor Koning leaned forward once more.

"Very red. The sign of internal suffocation. The blood retains its color." Then he looked around. "What's all this . . . a meeting of some sort?"

DeKok nodded.

"The ladies are all members of a spiritualists circle. There was a seance at the time. The universal opinion is that the woman was killed by an evil spirit . . . you know most of the rest."

With a gesture DeKok indicated the photographer who immediately started to take his shots. The other experts who always gathered at the scene of a murder, spread out. Some started dusting for fingerprints and some consulted about the order of interrogations of the witnesses. A uniformed constable stood by the door and DeKok knew that additional constables guarded the premises outside.

Dr. Koning gave DeKok a strange look.

"And you believe that?"

For a moment DeKok was at a loss.

"What, doctor?"

"The killing by an evil spirit," grumbled the old man.

DeKok smiled gently.

"Not at face value," he evaded the question. "I'm still trying to come to grips with the concept of an 'evil spirit.' But for the moment I'm more interested in knowing *how* this woman met her end."

The Coroner replaced his hat on his head. Then he took off his glasses. He fished a large, silk handkerchief from the breast pocket of his cutaway coat and carefully cleaned the glasses.

"Mmm," he said.

"Any ideas, doctor?" asked DeKok.

The old man carefully replaced his glasses on his nose and put away the handkerchief. He gave DeKok a long, hard look.

"You know, DeKok," he said, "that I don't like to give my opinion at this time. That should properly wait for the official autopsy."

"I know, doctor. But it would help me if you could give me a hint. I promise not to let it influence me."

"I don't know why I give in to you. You're the only one, you know."

"Thank you, doctor," said DeKok. He waited. "Well, doctor?" he prompted after a few seconds.

"Oh, very well," said the Coroner. "I'm almost convinced that the respiratory organ tissues that are responsible for separating the oxygen from the blood were paralyzed."

"And that means . . ."

"A gas . . . a poison."

"Which?"

"Really, DeKok," protested the old Coroner. "That's enough. I don't know and even if I knew I would not tell you. In fact, I've already told you more than I should have. Besides, only a thorough autopsy *and* a toxicological investigation will be able to isolate the reagent."

DeKok chewed his lower lip.

"It must have happened quickly."

"What do you mean?"

DeKok gestured.

"The woman was seated at the table with the others . . . happy and healthy. In any case, there were no indications that something was wrong with her. According to the initial statements, she suddenly gripped her throat, groaned, fell from the chair and died almost immediately."

Doctor Koning became interested.

"That is indeed fast," he said.

"Potassium Cyanide?"

The Coroner shook his head.

"You've read too much stuff by that fellow, what's his name, Baantjer," he said pensively. "Sometimes it's suggested that potassium cyanide is a fast-acting poison . . . and it *is*. But not so fast that someone will immediately drop dead. The time between ingestion of the poison and the onset of death is at least thirty minutes, maybe more, depending on the individual."

"Thirty minutes?"

"Indeed. I would be more inclined to think of a different type of cyanide. The kind that generates hydrocyanic acid gas."

DeKok swallowed.

"*Prussic* acid?"

"Yes."

DeKok looked surprised.

"I didn't smell anything."

"You mean the smell of bitter almonds?"

"Yes . . . that's what I mean."

"The cyanogens that are currently available are extremely fine grained. Immediately after dampening they transform into the feared hydrocyanic acid gas, or Prussic acid. Then, very briefly, it gives off the odor of bitter almonds." He pointed at the dead woman. "She used a strong perfume. Then other odors get drowned, so to speak."

DeKok cocked his head at the old doctor. He had seldom known him to be this loquacious. Usually almost every word that sounded like an opinion, had to be dragged out of him. He decided to take advantage of the rare opportunity to pick the doctor's brains. The old man had been a Coroner before DeKok joined the force and his wealth of experience was not to be disregarded.

"You mean there *could* have been a smell of bitter almonds?"

"Certainly."

The blind woman on the chair next to them stirred restlessly.

"That smell was present," she said tensely, "Bitter almonds. I'm sure of it. I smelled it . . . despite the perfume."

Both men turned toward Jennifer.

"You did?" they asked almost simultaneously.

Jennifer nodded positively.

"I smelled it," she repeated. "Ever since I became blind, my other senses seem to have grown stronger. I have excellent hearing and a fine nose."

DeKok leaned closer.

"When did you smell it?" he asked.

"Just before she fell from the chair." She hesitated. "Maybe . . . maybe the smell was there earlier as well."

"How much earlier?"

"That . . . that I don't know. If you hadn't mentioned the smell of almonds, I would probably have forgotten all about it. It seemed unimportant. It happens more often that I suddenly smell strange aromas."

DeKok came closer and whispered in her ear.

"Did you ever notice that smell in the house before?"

Jennifer pulled away from him, as if frightened.

"No, no. Certainly not."

Doctor Koning suddenly took his leave. He stopped near the door and turned around. With a graceful bow, reminiscent of a time long gone, he took off his hat.

"*Au revoir, mon ami,*" he called out. "My compliments to Dr. Rusteloos."

DeKok waved in farewell, reflecting that when the old doctor went to school, French was the language of choice at universities. He was genuinely fond of the old man and was grateful for his insight.

As soon as the Coroner had disappeared, the two morgue attendants stepped forward. They glanced at DeKok, who nodded. They placed the stretcher on the floor, unrolled the body bag and with calm, sure movements put the body in the bag and secured what was left of Black Julie on the stretcher.

"Where to?" asked the taller of the two, "Police lab?"

"Yes," said DeKok.

They lifted the stretcher and left. DeKok watched them go and wondered briefly how many corpses he had seen disappear that way, softly rocking between two unemotional people from the morgue. Hundreds? Or more? Perhaps he should keep a tally.

Vledder addressed him.

"Want me to go with them?"

"Make sure they undress her and take care of the clothes, especially the blouse. On the left breast was a spot . . . probably coffee and . . ." He stopped in mid-sentence. His face paled and he looked with astonishment at Vledder. "Coffee," he repeated, "Good grief . . . coffee . . . she drank coffee." He turned suddenly toward Christine Vanwal. "Where are the cups?"

The woman reacted surprised, uncertain.

"What . . . eh, *which* cups?"

DeKok snorted impatiently.

"The coffee cups . . . you had coffee, didn't you?"

Christine Vanwal gestured vaguely toward the back of the house. Her hand shook.

"In . . . eh, in . . . the kitchen."

DeKok raced out of the room, leaving Vledder and the women in astonished, but amused silence. DeKok at speed was a comical sight.

Still panting, he reached the kitchen. Defeated he stopped within a step after entering and narrowed his eyes. There was a large yellow tub in the granite sink and in the foaming water were ten porcelain cups and saucers.

* * *

DeKok paced up and down the detective room of Warmoes Street station. It was one of his habits. The friendly creases in his face had hardened and gave him the appearance of an angry mastiff. His lips were pressed together as he slapped his forehead with a flat hand.

"Stupid," he roared, "just plain stupid. I'll never forgive myself. I allowed myself to be distracted by the chattering of those women about ghosts and spirits. I should have immediately thought about that maledictive coffee." He slapped his forehead again. "As soon as I saw the brown spot on her blouse, I should have reacted."

Vledder came from behind his desk.

"Couldn't you have taken the cups from the tub?"

DeKok stopped his pacing and shook his head.

"That would have been useless. According to Harry Donkers he rinsed the cups before he put them in the soapy water. The chance that any poison remnants remain after that are minuscule. I certainly would not have sent anything *that* compromised to the lab. Also, the soap would probably have tainted any results into unacceptability."

Vledder nodded.

"I understand, you don't want some defense lawyer to get it thrown out because of a technicality."

DeKok nodded slowly.

"I'd rather wait for the toxicological examination of the body after the autopsy." He sighed "It will have to do . . . more's the pity. From a judicial point of view I would have been on more solid ground otherwise."

"How's that?"

"If I could prove that the poison came from one of the cups, I would narrow down the possible suspects."

"Of course. Didn't you think it a bit strange that Harry Donkers was so quick to rinse the cups?"

DeKok grinned without mirth.

"I can find it strange all I want. But what sort of proof is it? Harry Donkers just happens to be a neat person who abhors dirty dishes." He shook his head sadly. "You can't blame *him* that he did not see the connection between the coffee and the sudden death of Julie."

Vledder leaned against his desk.

"You're convinced the poison was mixed in the coffee?"

DeKok nodded.

"Yes, If we assume that Julie died of poisoning . . . and it certainly looks that way . . . then it must have been administered through the coffee. There is virtually no other possibility. And it happened during the second cup."

"Second cup?"

DeKok raised two fingers of his left hand.

"Coffee was served twice. The first time just before the beginning of the seance and the second time after the Ouija board, after the announcement that Jane was to die. Much to the annoyance of Christine Vanwal and Jennifer Jordan, Black Julie arrived late. She missed the first cup of coffee, Harry Donkers had already cleared away."

Vledder nodded slowly.

"You're right, of course." He remained silent and looked at his old mentor with a thoughtful look in his eyes. "But I don't think we have to despair. I think we can solve this case easily. No matter what, it's almost certain that one of the members of the circle must have administered the poison. And considering the fast action of the poison, it must have been administered in Jennifer's house. There's no other possibility. There were nine women in that canal house at the time . . . and one man. I double checked. Black Julie died, so that leaves nine suspects, eight women and a man." He paused. "Why don't we just arrest Harry Donkers right now? He had the best opportunity of all of them. He did not participate in the actual seance and there was nobody to watch him. He prepared the coffee both times and he was in the best possible position to add the poison to one cup. It would certainly explain why he was so eager to wash them as quickly as possible."

DeKok gave him an appreciative look.

"Very good," he said, approval in his voice. "A clear, concise analysis of the possibilities. There's little to refute it." He shook his head. "But I prefer to wait, nevertheless. It's a bit too early to think about arrests. Murder demands a motive. What sort of motive could Harry Donkers have to kill Black Julie? As far as we can explore that . . ."

He was interrupted by a scuffle near the door. Both DeKok and Vledder looked in the direction of the disturbance. One of the detectives near that end of the room tried to restrain a small, elderly woman. She had suddenly barged in and was headed for DeKok when the detective intercepted her. She wore an old-fashioned, shiny, black coat. The lapels and the sleeves were almost green with age. A broad straw hat, decorated with flowers perched precariously on the back of her head. The two Inspectors recognized her immediately and at a gesture from DeKok, she was allowed to proceed. DeKok approached her and held out his hand.

"Agatha Cologne," he said resignedly, "what gives us the pleasure of your company?"

She twisted her mouth into a hard line.

"It's no pleasure," she said sharply. "Polite words, but nothing more than a sham. I'm here on a mission. I'm here to rectify an ignominy, obliterate a disgrace."

"What sort of disgrace?"

She stuck out her pointed chin, a combative look in her eyes. There were rancorous lines around her mouth and nose.

"The disgrace of Julie's death," she said fervently. "It's a disgrace she was killed."

DeKok gently led her to a chair and urged her to sit down.

"I'm in complete agreement with you," he said calmly, earnestly. "It is indeed a disgrace. We must respect the lives of other people. I can assure you that we will do everything possible to find the murderer."

She gave him a pitiful smile.

"I'm afraid that is not nearly good enough." She shook her head decisively. "And . . . to tell the truth, I don't have a lot of faith in your methods. There are too many murders that remain unsolved."

DeKok swallowed.

"My colleague Vledder," he nodded in Vledder's direction, "and I have been able to achieve some modest successes. We're not exactly amateurs."

She shook her head again. Emphatically.

"You'll never unmask her. You can't." There was contempt in her creaky voice. "She's much too smart for you, too devious, too sly. It's not the first time she managed to get away with murder."

DeKok narrowed his eyes.

"Who are you talking about?"

Agatha Cologne leaned closer. Her wrinkled face with the fiercely gleaming eyes almost touched DeKok's face.

"About the murderess . . . the snake, the serpent who killed Black Julie, made her swallow poison."

DeKok licked his lips and leaned back.

"And you know who did it?"

There was a bitter grin on her face.

"Of course I know." She tapped herself on the hollow, bony chest. "Here . . . in my heart, there's no doubt at all. She's a devilish woman . . . spawned by rats."

"Who?"

She gave him a disdainful look.

"That Annette . . . that Annette Leeuwenhoek. And she knows exactly how to go about it."

4

DeKok stood up and started to pace up and down behind his desk. After a while he stopped and looked down on the seated woman. The straw hat, he thought, was conflicting ludicrously with the rest of her appearance, which bespoke proud, though impoverished gentility.

"That's a serious accusation," he said gravely. "I take it that you are fully aware of what you just said."

Agatha Cologne looked up at him. The look in her eyes was as fierce as before and her face had a dogged look.

"Of course I know," she said sharply. "I'm not senile. I didn't come here to tell you a story, a fantasy. Annette Leeuwenhoek killed her first husband in cold blood. She had been messing around for some time with the character she's married to now. But her own husband was just too good, too trusting . . . a lunk who didn't believe in divorce."

"Thus . . . he had to disappear?"

She laughed falsely.

"Good guess, Mister Inspector. She was determined to have the other man. She wanted to marry him. That's why her own husband had to disappear and when he didn't want to cooperate, she helped him along. You understand, Inspector? In less than a week she had rid herself of him, without so much as a hint of regret."

"How do you know that?"

She pointed a finger at the ceiling.

"My own sister, Martha . . . I lost her this week." She made a cross. "God rest her soul. A few days before she died, she told me everything."

DeKok's eyebrows danced across his forehead, but only Vledder enjoyed the show. Agatha was too wrapped up in self-righteous indignation to observe the phenomenon.

"And how did your sister Martha gain such knowledge?"

Agatha moved in her chair and giggled like an adolescent.

"From Black Julie . . . *she* knew about it. She knew everything . . . from soup to nuts. She was married to a brother of Annette Leeuwenhoek and experienced the demise of the first husband from close by." She grinned, which made her look like a witch. "*Now* do you understand why Julie had to die. Black Julie told everyone who'd listen that Annette had killed her first husband.

DeKok was shocked.

"How long ago did that happen?"

"Twelve years ago."

"And why did Julie not notify the police?"

Agatha Cologne snorted contemptuously.

"The police? Whatever for? She came here once, to Warmoes Street, but nobody took her seriously."

DeKok pretended not to have heard the last comment. Such criticism, he knew, was too often just a perception. Thoughtfully, he rubbed the back of his neck.

"How . . . eh, how did Annette kill her husband?"

Agatha waved her arms theatrically.

"The same as with Julie . . . with poison."

* * *

When the diminutive, and above all else, spiteful Agatha Cologne had left, there fell a deep silence between Vledder and DeKok. It was as if their small part of the detective room had suddenly been encapsulated into a cone of silence. The constant background noise from the room, the phones and the busy murmur from the street outside, did not seem to penetrate.

DeKok leaned his elbows on his desk, his chin supported by his hands. His face was somber and deep creases carved his forehead.

"Who could possibly gain," he sighed, "from Black Julie's death?"

Vledder grinned light-heartedly.

"If we could answer *that* question," he said, "then we would have solved the case."

DeKok looked at his partner for several long seconds.

"You're extremely sharp today," he said finally. "I need a vacation. I feel it. I'll propose to the Commissaris that you can solve this one on your own."

Vledder's face fell.

"I'm not all that sharp," he admitted.

DeKok smiled thinly.

"When is the autopsy?"

"Tomorrow, at eleven. That's the earliest time Dr. Rusteloos is available. It's busy this time of year, he said. He had another autopsy out of town to take care of."

DeKok nodded his understanding.

"Murder," he said cynically, "is a business without malaise, even in our little country." He looked at Vledder. "Julie's blouse went to the lab?"

"Yes, Dr. Eskes only worried that the spot might be too small to give him an acceptable analysis. But he promised to try."

DeKok leaned back and placed his feet on the desk.

"Well, we haven't made a very good start," he said in a depressed tone of voice. "We have already made one major mistake and we know little else. What exactly do we know about Black Julie. I mean, apart from the information obtained from Town Hall, where she is listed as Jane Truffle. Did you find out anything else?"

Vledder pulled out his notebook and with the same movement angled the screen of his computer terminal toward himself. He had already entered all pertinent information into his computer, but still, like a good cop, he consulted his notebook as well. DeKok had impressed on him too often that a cop's notebook, which recorded first, initial impressions, was far preferable to electronic memories which were too often subject to editing when entered. DeKok's own computer terminal gathered dust on the corner of his desk. Vledder was certain that Dekok had no idea where the power switch was. The only time Vledder had seen DeKok use the computer, it was to shade the face of a baby from the harsh overhead lights.* DeKok did not like modern technology and avoided it as much as possible.

DeKok had originally joined a force that moved on foot, or by bicycle and, when in a hurry, took a streetcar, or a taxi. The fastest communication had been with the use of lock-boxes, many of which were not equipped with a phone, but only allowed a limited number of standard messages. DeKok never tired of pointing out that, during the 17th Century the Dutch had controlled a world-wide empire when the fastest communication was by sailing ship. He was firmly convinced that the empire broke down because of instant communications, which killed initiative in people on the spot and concentrated the decision

---

* See: *DeKok and the Dancing Death.*

making process with a few, cautious people in the main offices of the various companies.

All this went through Vledder's mind as he flipped to the appropriate pages of his notebook.

"According to my information," he said, answering DeKok's question, "she was born in the Jordaan, the daughter of a barrel organ grinder who was more often drunk than not and a mother who still prostituted herself while pregnant."

"Well, well," said DeKok, rubbing his chin.

"It was a completely a-social household," added Vledder.

"And the appellation 'Black Julie' makes me suspect," said DeKok sadly, "that Jane Truffle was not unfamiliar with the Red Light District herself."

Vledder raised a hand in protest.

"Not so fast. As a young girl she was conspicuous for her . . . eh, her exuberant figure." He grinned. "It must have been something remarkable, indeed. It's probably the reason she was hired as a waitress in one of the brothels along Thorbecke Square, you know, where all the waiters and waitresses are nude. Anyway, she worked there for years. During her twenty-seventh year she married Charles Leeuwenhoek, a rather wild young man, who at pa's expense led the life of a playboy and the eternal student."

"Annette's brother."

Vledder nodded.

"Exactly . . . Annette's brother. It was a stormy marriage that lasted barely five years when Charles, according to him, caught his better half in an extra-marital escapade. He immediately showed her the door."

"And the marriage was dissolved?"

Vledder shook his head.

"That's the strange bit. The marriage is still valid. Apparently Julie, or Jane as we should call her, fought a divorce with tooth and nail."

"But why?"

Vledder made a helpless gesture.

"She said she liked the name Leeuwenhoek . . . it was too nice, too distinguished to relinquish."

"Distinguished?"

"Sure, you remember Anthony van Leeuwenhoek, the inventor of the microscope and the discoverer of red blood corpuscles."

"Good grief, that was in the 1600s. Surely she didn't think she was related?"

"No, of course not. As I said, she just *liked* the name."

"Really? Sounds a bit cynical to me."

Vledder grinned.

"Perhaps. I was unable to find out. I think she wanted to keep the name because of the child."

DeKok looked up, surprised.

"Child?"

Vledder nodded.

"A son, Richard. The boy is now about fourteen."

"A child by Charles?'

"That," smiled Vledder, "is how he's registered in the Records of Births and Deaths."

"Where is the boy?"

Vledder shrugged.

"Nobody knows. Jane always kept him away from the Leeuwenhoek family. Nobody could even give me a description of the boy."

DeKok grimaced.

"Well, it certainly explains why Annette Leeuwenhoek isn't too thrilled with her sister-in-law."

Vledder nodded agreement.

"That's indeed the case. But according to Christine Vanwal, Annette was just a little too much of a lady to express her disapproval openly. That's why it was possible for both of them to be members of the same spiritualists circle."

DeKok chewed his lower lip.

"What did Jane do after the separation from Charles?"

Again Vledder consulted his notebook. But he also cast a quick glance at his computer screen before answering.

"She had several affairs after that. Fleeting relationships. Too short, in any case, to enable us to find out the names of the men involved. But for the last eight years or so, she's been living with an invalid construction worker about whom nothing is known in our files."

DeKok looked doubtful.

"What's his name?"

"Gerard . . . Gerard Klaver. He's forty-seven. They have been living for some time in the village of Landsmeer, Foxtail Street . . . a new development with single family residences."

"What did she live on?"

"He has a disability pension, which may be adequate. And Black Julie helped out. She had a regular group of clients, consisting of lonely old men whom she visited from time to time . . . obviously in exchange for some sort of compensation."

DeKok smiled.

"I suspected something like that. The old gentlemen will now await her with desire, but for nought." He paused and then gave Vledder a long, hard look. "That's a lot of information in a short time. How did you manage that?"

Vledder smirked.

"Mathilda Lochem."

"And who is Mathilda Lochem?"

Vledder waved carelessly.

"A shrewd old lady . . . the Miss Marple type. Very interesting and . . . interested. She's one of the members of the group that regularly met at Jennifer Jordan's house. You should go see her. She loves to talk."

DeKok rubbed the bridge of his nose with a little finger.

"Does Mathilda Lochem also suspect Annette Leeuwenhoek of having committed murder?"

Vledder hesitated.

"I didn't discuss that with her. I just inquired about the background of Black Julie. That seemed to be important at the time. After all," he defended himself, "somewhere in her life *must* be a clue as to why she was killed."

DeKok sighed elaborately.

"Maybe . . . but I have the sinking feeling that there's a lot more to this affair than we can possibly fathom at this time."

Vledder made an entry on his computer and then half turned around to his partner.

"Do you think Black Julie was here, in this station, with her story?"

"The accusation that Annette had poisoned her husband?"

"Yes."

DeKok shrugged.

"We'll have to ask Aad, our much under-appreciated Chief of Administration, to check it out. If she was here, whether action was taken or not, there should be a record. But I find it hard to believe. I was already on the murder squad at that time and I think I would have heard. But apart from that, even a rookie would have taken notice of an accusation involving poison."

Vledder stretched out a hand toward his partner.

"But, it could have been a motive for murder, just like Agatha Cologne said."

DeKok looked quizzical.

"After twelve years?"

"What do you mean?"

DeKok spread both hands in a gesture of surrender.

"For twelve years Black Julie has been able to spread the rumor far and wide that her sister-in-law committed murder . . . and now . . . all of sudden, Annette would . . ." He did not complete the sentence. "There can be other motives, motives we don't even suspect at this time." He paused again. "In the annals of crime it's well known that a person who successfully killed once with poison, isn't apprehensive about doing it again." He grinned without joy. "It's almost an addiction. Most poisoners in the past had cemeteries full of victims."

Vledder gave a short, barking laugh.

"But what about the clear accusation by Agatha. We can hardly ignore it."

DeKok rubbed his eyes.

"You're right," he agreed. "We're practically obligated to investigate if Annette Leeuwenhoek did indeed kill her first husband."

"After twelve years?"

"Yes," nodded DeKok. "There's no statute of limitations on murder. Annette Leeuwenhoek can still face judicial prosecution. The question is . . . can we still prove it?"

"Exhumation?"

DeKok shook his head, looking doubtful.

"That's not so simple. We must have reasonable . . . *strong* suspicions before a Judge-Advocate will give permission for an exhumation. In fact, you should know beforehand what sort of poison was used."

"How's that?"

DeKok gestured.

"By poisons that filter rapidly through the body," he explained, "exhumation is senseless. You must have a reasonable chance of isolating the poison from the remains of the suspected victim."

Vledder sank his head in his hands.

"I think we're stirring up a hornet's nest."

DeKok lifted his legs from the desk, a faint smile on his lips. He nodded at his young colleague.

"That, my boy," he said, "is to put it mildly. If the signs weren't . . ."

He stopped as the door to the detective room was suddenly thrown open. Commissaris* Buitendam, the tall, stately chief of Warmoes Street Station stood in the door opening. His white silk scarf was knotted carelessly on top of his overcoat. With a crooked finger he motioned toward DeKok to follow him, then he turned on his heels and walked away in the direction of his own office.

DeKok followed him, slowly, calmly, uninterested. When he arrived at the office, the Commissaris was already seated behind his desk. The usually pale commissarial face was red with excitement and his nostrils quivered in anger.

"Why," he roared, "did I not know about the murder?"

DeKok looked at him unemotionally.

"What murder?"

The Commissaris wildly waved his arms.

"That woman . . . during the seance."

DeKok made what could be interpreted as an apologetic gesture.

"You were not in the station when the call came through. And you weren't here when Vledder and I returned from our preliminary investigation. Thus I authorized an extensive telex message with all particulars." He scratched the back of his neck

---

* A rank equivalent to Captain.

while the Commissaris, slightly calmer, reflected that only DeKok still spoke of telex messages when those had long since been replaced by faxes and instant inter-net communications between computers. "But perhaps," continued DeKok, "you don't read telex messages ... I must say, a dangerous and detrimental dereliction of duty ... for a Commissaris."

The momentary calm fled before the storm of Buitendam's new anger.

"I didn't have time to read any telex messages," he yelled. "I was at Princes Canal."

"Oh?" queried DeKok, knowing full well that it was the common reference for the Palace of Justice, which was located on the prestigious canal.

"Yes," shouted his Chief. "I was in a meeting with Maitre Lochem, the Judge-Advocate and I had to hear from *him* that a murder had been committed in *my* district. The Judge-Advocate showed surprise that I didn't know."

DeKok cocked his head at the Commissaris.

"Ah, so the Judge-Advocate *did* have time to read telex messages."

"I ... I don't think so," blustered the Commissaris.

"But he was in the same meeting?"

"Yes, he chaired the meeting."

DeKok showed a mixture of surprise and skepticism.

"Then ... how did he know?"

"From his sister ... Mathilda Lochem. An elderly lady, but quite active. She had him called out of the meeting. She was a witness when that woman died during the spiritualists seance. And she also had a proposal with which the Judge-Advocate immediately agreed."

DeKok looked suspicious.

"A proposal?"

Buitendam nodded emphatically.

"Tomorrow night that circle will hold another seance. Mathilda Lochem has already organized that. The Judge-Advocate and I have been invited to attend."

"To do what?"

Buitendam reacted nonchalantly.

"To ask questions of the spirit of the murdered woman."

5

For a moment DeKok was stunned. His mouth fell open and he stared at the Commissaris as if he was something from another planet. Then he shook his head in despair.

"And you *both* accepted the invitation?"

The Commissaris nodded.

"Certainly. Of course, we have. I agree with Maitre Lochem: this is indeed a unique opportunity to experience the atmosphere at such a seance. Perhaps it will help us get closer to the murderer."

DeKok swallowed.

"With the help of the ghost of the deceased?"

There was amazement, disbelief and incredulity in his voice.

The Commissaris gave him a hard look. He had noticed the tone of voice.

"Yes, I . . . indeed," said the Chief hesitantly. "Yes, perhaps with the help of the spirit of the deceased. On the face of it, it may seem a bit absurd . . . but, eh, perhaps she has since discovered who was responsible for her death."

DeKok grinned bitterly.

"How?"

The Commissaris did not understand what he meant and looked it.

"What do you mean?"

DeKok gestured wildly.

"How will the ghost of the murdered woman have discovered that?"

The Commissaris moved uneasily in his chair.

"Yes, well . . . that, I don't know," he said slowly. "Personally I'm not, I mean I'm not personally very familiar with the spirit world. But the Judge-Advocate feels that there are real possibilities. According to his sister, Mathilda, there have been remarkable results in the past."

DeKok snorted.

"Mathilda Lochem," he said, contempt in his voice, ". . . an old busybody, a rich old lady suffering from delusions and fantasies. Perhaps she's got nothing better to do with her spare time but to occupy herself with such . . . such charlatanism. I can understand that. But that a Dutch Judge-Advocate and an Amsterdam Commissaris of Police seriously consider such hocus-pocus to be of any value and then agree to . . . to cooperate! It's not only amazing . . . it's amazingly stupid."

The commissarial face hardened.

"That," he almost stuttered, "is . . . is an uncalled for remark."

DeKok stared him down.

"You're right," he said finally, "it is."

The Commissaris slammed his fist on the desk.

"Your superiors," he roared angrily, "are not stupid."

DeKok raised his hands in a defensive gesture.

"Excuse me," he said with a sigh, "I always thought the same. But now I discover, much to my chagrin, that I was wrong all along."

Commissaris Buitendam lost his last little bit of patience. With an angry face he jumped up from his chair and pointed at the door with a shaking hand.

"OUT!"

DeKok left.

* * *

Vledder smiled.

"I heard the yell," he said. "You're disagreeing again. Why, why? You owe respect to your very own Commissaris. It says something like that in the standing orders. Anyway, after all these years you really should be more concerned about his blood pressure. One of these days he'll have a heart attack and you'll be to blame."

DeKok ignored the remarks and sank in his chair.

"Forget it, will you, Dick? I don't agree with it, but I can understand it when the man is misguided. After all, all he worries about is the end of his career and his pension. He just doesn't want to make waves. I've lived with it in the past and I can do it again. But there is a difference between being misguided and being plain stupid."

"Stupid?" asked Vledder.

"Yes, stupid. They're going to have a special seance to call on the ghost of Black Julie."

"Who?"

"That circle, Jennifer's spiritualist group. And they have invited our Commissaris and the Judge-Advocate as special guests. If the ghost of Black Julie then appears, they can ask her a few questions and solve the murder at the same time."

Vledder grinned from ear to ear.

"You're kidding, right?"

"No, I'm not in the mood for jokes."

"But that's marvelous, DeKok." Vledder could not let it go. "What fools we've been all these years. Hunting all over the place, looking for clues, painfully building a theory and then, with luck, sometimes even catching the perpetrator. What a waste of time. From now on, every time we find a corpse, we'll immediately have a seance and the case is solved."

DeKok looked grim.

"Enough is enough. It seems that your friend, Mathilda Lochem, has arranged it all."

"She's not *my* friend," growled Vledder.

DeKok rubbed the bridge of his nose with a little finger.

"You seemed quite charmed by her," he said innocently.

Vledder shrugged with annoyance.

"I thought her to be a bright, alert old lady who noticed things. That's all."

DeKok gave him a denigrating grin.

"But she's capable of being in our way. In any case, she has enough influence over her brother, the Judge-Advocate, that he immediately agreed to her proposal for a new seance."

Vledder frowned.

"And with Jennifer Jordan as the medium?"

DeKok pushed his lower lip forward, it gave him a surprisingly pouting appearance.

"It wasn't said in so many words, but I assume so. According to those who can know, Jennifer Jordan is a particularly effective medium. Besides, who else could they find on such short notice?"

"But she refused to call on the spirit of Martha Cologne because she had died so recently." DeKok smiled. "Well," continued Vledder, "that's exactly my point. Black Julie's death is of an even more recent date."

DeKok nodded thoughtfully.

"Perhaps Jennifer is under the influence of your friend Mathilda as well."

Vledder came to his feet, irritation on his face.

"I told you: she isn't *my* friend. I really don't care for old busybodies who are forever sticking their noses where they don't belong."

"What happened to the alert old lady?" teased DeKok.

Vledder came from behind his desk, ignoring the question. He leaned against DeKok's desk.

"What are we going to do?" he asked, a challenge in his voice.

"Whatever do you mean?"

"Are we also going to that seance?"

DeKok shook his head decisively.

"No way. Not a hair on my head could persuade me."

"Why not?"

DeKok sighed deeply.

"Please understand," he said patiently, "I have nothing against spiritualism and even less against the people who believe in it. As my old mother used to say: *Investigate all things and retain that which is worthy.* And if it wasn't my duty to investigate a murder, I wouldn't mind, as a private citizen, you understand ... I wouldn't mind attending a seance. But *professionally*, I can't afford to get involved. And I find the plans of the Commissaris and the Judge-Advocate, to say the least, irresponsible."

"Why?"

DeKok spread wide his arms.

"Let's just assume for a moment that tomorrow night the ghost of Black Julie does indeed materialize and that this *ghost* accuses Annette Leeuwenhoek of murdering her. Then what? What can anyone do with such an accusation. What use is it to the Commissaris, or the Judge-Advocate. Nothing, less than nothing. They can hardly arrest Annette and have her appear in court on the testimony of a ghost. You understand? Perhaps Black Julie is a fine ghostly presence, but one will need *reasonable*, that is *earthly* proof before a Dutch judge will convict, or even consider the evidence, for that matter."

"So a seance is nothing but hocus-pocus?"

DeKok shook his head.

"I wouldn't go as far as that," he said earnestly, "despite what I said to the Commissaris. Perhaps, just perhaps, it *is* possible to contact the spirit world, to speak with the departed. I wouldn't know, I certainly wouldn't judge. I do insist, however, that *personally*, as a police Inspector, I keep both feet firmly on the ground and my head *out* of the clouds."

Vledder looked at the large, raw-boned figure of his friend, a smile on his lips.

"Not difficult, for a man with your measurements," teased Vledder.

DeKok laughed comfortably and leaned back in his chair.

"You know, Dick," he continued in a didactic tone, "as a cop I've always been wary of the supernatural. I've never, of my own free will, used prognosticators, clairvoyants, para-psychologists, or whatever they call that sort of experts. The few times that I *have* worked with them, it was always on the express insistence of the family of the victim . . . people who *did* believe in the effectiveness of such practitioners."

"But you don't believe it?"

DeKok shook his head slowly.

"No. They've never been able to convince me. Despite the often complimentary articles in newspapers and some magazines . . . I always found the results either to be expected, or less than could have been obtained with proper police work."

Vledder gestured.

"Perhaps you've always been unlucky . . . perhaps in your case the occult . . . eh, atmosphere was less than favorable."

DeKok stared into the distance.

"Maybe, but I can't forget Houdini."

"Houdini? The escape artist?"

"Yes, he was also an accomplished magician, however, and used to fooling the public . . . on a stage, or in a theatrical setting. But he made it his life's work to expose spiritualists as charlatans."

"Did he succeed?"

"Not entirely, but then, the other side never advanced convincing arguments that they were *not*."

Suddenly DeKok stood up and walked over to the coat rack. Vledder followed him.

"Where are we going?"

DeKok hoisted himself in his old, threadbare raincoat and perched his ridiculous, little felt hat on his head.

"To Landsmeer."

"To see Gerard Klaver?"

"That's right, Julie's friend."

Vledder walked past him and held open the door.

"What for?" asked the young man.

DeKok walked down the hall toward the stairs and answered over his shoulder.

"To ask if Black Julie ever talked to him in bed." Suddenly he stopped, a smile on his face. "Or, perhaps Black Julie wasn't the kind of woman who talked a lot in bed."

* * *

"In that case you're mistaken. Jane loved to talk in bed, for hours. She used to get real upset with me if I turned around to try and sleep. Then it wouldn't take much or we'd quarrel. Just one wrong word . . ." He smiled tenderly. "She wasn't the sort of woman you'd want to fight with it. Great Scot, she could carry on so . . . unbelievable. And stubborn . . . like a mule . . . once she didn't talk to me for three months."

"You loved her?"

The rough-hewn face of Gerard Klaver sobered. There was a sad smile on his face. He swallowed and his adam's apple bobbed nervously up and down.

"She . . . she was everything to me. Jane. I loved her . . . and she loved me. Truly, with all her heart. She was so beautiful . . . so very beautiful. The most beautiful girl in the world . . . always was." He shook his head. "I know what people thought about her. She was no good, they said. She was not to be trusted." he lowered his head and sobbed softly. "But nobody knew her, nobody knew her the way I knew her. For me . . . for me, she was a darling . . . a . . ." He was unable to go on. Tears came down his cheeks, dripped on his hands.

DeKok let him be. It was sad to see this strong, big man cry like a child. Meanwhile DeKok wondered why Black Julie had been attracted to this man. He wasn't handsome in the traditional way. On the contrary, a large, rough face, jutting cheekbones and narrow, deep eyes gave the face a somewhat sinister look. The head was crowned by a large, unruly mop of reddish hair.

DeKok leaned closer.

"She married someone else."

Gerard Klaver looked up. He used a sleeve of his shirt to dry his eyes.

"Charles . . . Charles Leeuwenhoek." Scorn colored his voice. "A slimy sorta guy. Dirty, stupid, but rich."

"It wasn't a marriage of love?"

Gerard Klaver snorted derisively. He was clearly getting excited. His cheeks regained some color.

"Love . . . Jane . . . for such a . . . a weak customer?" He shook his head. "She abhorred him . . . hated him. She hated every atom of his being."

DeKok gave him a searching look.

"But yet she married him."

Gerard raked his fingers through his hair without straightening it out in the least. But he seemed calmer.

"For me," he said.

"For you?"

"And for our child."

"*Your* child?"

Klaver nodded again, sighing deeply.

"The child of Jane and me." He looked at DeKok, calm, relaxed. "I see you don't understand. Perhaps you don't believe me. But it's true. Jane married Charles for me, for me and our unborn child." He paused to lend emphasis to the words. "We had big plans for our child. Especially if it were to be a boy. University . . . engineer, lawyer, doctor . . . something like that. Big and important." He pressed his hands together in front of his face, repressed another onset of tears. "Let's face it, Jane and I, we come from the gutter . . . it's true. Jane's father drank like a Templar and her mother was pregnant every year. Plain poverty and misery. Jane never had a childhood . . . a youth. She had to work at a young age to help keep the family going. At my house it wasn't much different. You understand? Jane and I wanted something better for our child."

DeKok nodded his understanding, compassion in his eyes.

"She married Charles Leeuwenhoek to guarantee the education of the boy."

Klaver bit his lower lip.

"Perhaps she wouldn't have done it, if I hadn't fallen from the scaffolding." He slapped his right knee. "Stiff . . . forever useless. It happened just when we knew that Jane was pregnant."

He sighed deeply. "That Charles Leeuwenhoek had been sniffing around Jane for some time . . . after all, she worked in a public place and you know how the staff was dressed there, or rather, undressed. He always insisted on having Jane as his personal waitress. She had no choice, of course. She wasn't part of the staff that served the bedrooms, but still . . . she told me that when he was around, it was the only time she really felt naked, when she was working. She couldn't stand him, he made her vomit, she used to say. And she told him so. But when I had the accident and it was certain I would forever be an invalid, she decided to marry him."

"A marriage of convenience."

"Yes."

"For the money?"

The strong, crippled man balled his fists.

"I was against it. But what could I say? An invalid with a barely adequate pension. That's when I started to drink. She cursed me day and night. One night when I was drunk again, she walked out. She married the guy within days."

DeKok rubbed his chin.

"The marriage didn't last long."

Klaver chuckled smugly.

"She couldn't stay there."

"Why not?"

"The child . . . Richard."

"What was the matter with him?"

He grinned openly, a gleam in his eyes.

"The child looked more and more like his real father." He bowed his head and pulled his hair. "Red . . . this kind of red is unmistakable. Richard has the same kind of hair and the Leeuwenhoeks were starting to whisper. There had never been a redhead in the family. Besides, it was a 'seven-month' baby, you know. The family pressed for a divorce, but Jane wasn't about to give in. When the family became too bothersome, Jane took the child and had it raised elsewhere."

"And she left Charles?"

Klaver nodded. His mild expression changed and his face became a hard mask.

"Then they started."

"The Leeuwenhoek family?"

"Exactly . . . their true nature came to the fore, then, their criminal nature. At first they refused to provide for the child. It wasn't Charles' child, they maintained. But the child was registered in *his* name. Legally they didn't have a leg to stand on. Only after Jane threatened them with a scandal, did they start to pay up. But from that time on, Jane didn't have a moment's peace."

"How's that?"

Klaver took a deep breath.

"Murder attempts."

DeKok swallowed.

"Murder attempts?" he repeated, confused.

Klaver nodded slowly.

"The Leeuwenhoeks . . . they have tried to kill her at least five times."

6

They left Foxtail Street and the village of Landsmeer. Gerard Klaver, mused DeKok, a bitter man full of hate and thoughts of vengeance. DeKok had the uneasy feeling he would meet him again, that his role in this case was not played out. With a last wave, they turned the corner and headed back to Amsterdam.

Vledder, of course, was behind the wheel and he needed all his attention to manoeuvre through the busy traffic in the narrow main street of the village. DeKok slid down in his seat, completely confident in Vledder's ability to get them where they were going in one piece.

DeKok's face was expressionless as he searched his pockets. Finally he found a roll of peppermints and absent-mindedly put one in his mouth. He thought about what they had learned. Despite his long years with the police, DeKok, like most good cops, liked people. Although he usually came into contact with the dark underside of society, he was always genuinely moved when confronted with human suffering. It was obvious that Jane Truffle had known little happiness. Her violent death was a sad conclusion of her eventful life.

He pushed himself up and looked at the fields, separated by drainage ditches and at the miniature bridges, hardly wide enough for a single car. This part of Holland, like most of it, was also below sea level. In the distance he saw some windmills and he could clearly observe the current in the drainage ditches caused by the actions of the distant windmills. In Holland windmills usually pump water, part of the eternal battle to keep Holland dry and free of floods.

His thoughts drifted back to Jane Truffle. What was the motive for her murder? Who found it necessary that Jane die so quickly. An angry spirit . . . according to Jennifer Jordan . . . the spirit manifested itself clearly . . . again, according to the medium. But he, DeKok, did not like occult business. And he only believed in angry spirits as long as they still occupied the concrete, physical human form. The Leeuwenhoek family . . . according to Gerard Klaver . . . they have a bad spirit . . . a criminal nature.

DeKok rubbed his chin, crunching his peppermint. Who were the Leeuwenhoeks? What motivated them? A family conspiracy because of a failed marriage and a child born out of wedlock? Money is power. It was still true, as it had always been.

Vledder entered the outskirts of Amsterdam and looked at DeKok. The young man seemed to guess what DeKok was thinking.

"What happens to Richard?"

DeKok shrugged.

"I did not want to ask Klaver where the child was hidden. It seemed wrong, somehow. Besides, I don't think he would have told me . . . not just like that. I'm sure Charles Leeuwenhoek will turn to the Juvenile Protection Service. He *is* completely justified in demanding that the child be located. After all, *legally* he is the father. And, as far as I know, he has not been denied custody."

"But he could have demanded the child while Black Julie was still alive."

"Sure. He could have asked Juvenile Police, or the Juvenile Courts. He could have filed a formal law suit. Cases like that always involve a lot of emotions . . . and publicity. Perhaps the Leeuwenhoeks were reluctant to start judicial procedures. It's difficult, under our present system, to force a mother to reveal the location of her child . . . especially if she isn't disposed to do so in the first place."

Vledder entered the Harbor Tunnel.

"You believe that? About the murder attempts?"

"Well, according to Gerard Klaver, Jane never notified the police about any of those alleged attempts. Therefore there has never been an *official* inquiry." DeKok grimaced as he emphasized the word. "How much truth there is to the allegations, I mean, if they *really* planned to kill her . . . I don't know. I'm afraid that only Jane herself could have enlightened us on that point."

"But she's dead," said Vledder, curtly.

DeKok chewed his lower lip, staring.

"If the Leeuwenhoeks are indeed as dangerous as Klaver intimated," he said thoughtfully, "the child is in danger, too."

"The child?" Vledder sounded surprised.

DeKok tapped the dashboard for emphasis.

"The Leeuwenhoeks are a rich family. They might object to having a part of their wealth diverted to a child who, in their eyes, is no more than a bastard . . . an illegitimate child which they were tricked into accepting as part of the family . . ." He paused, nodded to himself. "Also, we should keep in mind that, as far as the family is concerned, Jane Truffle is no more than a sneaky liar, who callously exploited the heartfelt feelings of their Charles."

Vledder's mouth fell open.

"But that's a motive for murder," he exclaimed finally.

DeKok nodded slowly.

"Yes, my boy, it could well be."

* * *

Vledder parked the car in the secondary lot near the Damrak. From there they sauntered to Warmoes Street station. It was getting on dusk and there was a steady drizzle. The colorful neon signs in Old Bridge Alley and elsewhere reflected from the wet pavement. DeKok pushed his hat further down on his forehead and pulled up the collar of his raincoat. He returned the greeting from a prostitute with a smile and another greeting from a pimp with a curt nod. He waved at Moshe, the herring man, as they stepped through the front door of the station house.

"DeKok!!"

Meindert Post, the Watch Commander roared from his place behind the railing. The man had a voice as loud as a foghorn and even his whispers could be heard throughout the room. His ancestors, like DeKok's, had been fishermen on the former Zuyder Zee and no doubt the volume of his voice was a genetic remnant of the time when his family communicated through weather and storm from one boat to another on what had been one of the most treacherous bodies of water in the world.

"DeKok!" repeated Post in a lower volume, when he noticed that the old man had heard him.

The gray sleuth came closer.

"What's up?"

"There's a man waiting for you, upstairs."

"What sort of a man?"

"I don't know. He didn't mention his name and I didn't ask. You know the chaos here. I just sent him up."

"How long has he been waiting?"

The Watch Commander glanced at the clock.

"About forty-five minutes. I told him it might take a while before you were back."

"And?"

"He said he had plenty of time."

DeKok grinned.

"A remarkable man . . . in this busy age."

The two Inspectors walked through the restricted part of the front office toward the stairs in the back. In the corridor leading to the detective room they found a man on the long bench. DeKok estimated him to be in his late forties. He was neatly dressed, almost distinguished, with a gray coat and a white, silk scarf. An expensive Homburg was on the bench next to him. As soon as he saw the Inspectors, he picked up his hat and walked toward them.

"You . . . eh, you're Inspector DeKok?"

"Yes," said DeKok, "with kay-oh-kay." He pointed aside. "My colleague, Vledder."

The man shook hands.

"My name is Charles Leeuwenhoek. I wanted to talk to you about the sudden demise of my . . . my wife." He coughed discreetly behind his hand. "I take it that I have reached the right people to arrange the . . . the interment?"

DeKok nodded resignedly and led the way to the detective room. Leeuwenhoek seemed momentarily taken aback by the noise level in the room, but then he followed DeKok to his desk. At the desk DeKok stopped and shook hands again.

"Our sincere condolences," he said formally.

"Yes, yes . . ." stammered Leeuwenhoek. "Condolences . . . indeed. Thank you . . . thank you, indeed."

DeKok pointed at the chair next to his desk.

"Please sit down."

Leeuwenhoek pulled up the slips of his coat and sat down. He placed his Homburg on his knees.

"I understand that her . . . her passing has your . . . that you're interested in her passing?"

DeKok sat down behind his desk.

"In a professional way, yes," he said calmly. "She was murdered."

Leeuwenhoek moved in his chair, ill at ease.

"That's what I have been told, yes." His voice sounded nervous. "However . . . I can hardly, I can hardly believe it."

"You're surprised by her death?"

Charles Leeuwenhoek nodded vehemently.

"Especially in this way. What did you expect. It's . . . it's horrible. According to my sister . . ." He looked up. "Did you meet her?"

"We met her," confirmed DeKok. "As we met the other members of the spiritualists circle. Briefly. I regret that I have not yet had the opportunity to converse with her more in depth."

Charles Leeuwenhoek smiled.

"You should," he said enthusiastically. "She's a very intelligent woman and I always have received a lot of . . . a lot of support from her. As a matter of fact, ever since Father has become less active, physically as well as mentally, Annette has been the head of the family. Very resourceful and decisive, I must say."

DeKok nodded to himself. Meanwhile he observed his visitor sharply. He looked at the face. Gerard Klaver's description seemed a bit exaggerated. Charles Leeuwenhoek did not seem to be as weak as the former construction worker had described him. The pointed nose and the round, red cheeks gave the face a slightly puffy expression. But that was misleading. The gray-green eyes were clear and alert.

"What did your sister think?" asked DeKok with a winning smile.

Leeuwenhoek swallowed suddenly.

"Poison . . . poison. Apparently Julie's life was taken by poison."

DeKok nodded thoughtfully.

"Poison . . . that must have been administered in that canal house. That is why all . . . *all* the members of that spiritualistic group are under suspicion." He paused and leaned forward. His face was expressionless when he added: "Including your sister, Annette."

Leeuwenhoek pulled back and grinned nervously.

"That is . . . is absurd. Simply ridiculous."

DeKok gave him a penetrating look.

"You think so?"

Charles Leeuwenhoek half rose from his chair. His hat fell on the ground. He waved his arms.

"Of course, I think so. Why . . . why would Annette do such a thing? That . . . that is *insane!*"

DeKok remained unmoved.

"Murder," he said, "is insane."

Leeuwenhoek reached down and picked up his hat. Then he stood up.

"I have nothing more to say to you," he said in an arrogant tone of voice.

Vledder came closer. He had listened to the exchange and had become increasingly excited. He pushed Leeuwenhoek back in his chair.

"The members of that circle," said Vledder sharply, "knew Black Julie only casually. Just from the weekly seances. Other than that, there was practically no social intercourse . . . certainly not enough of an association which could lead to murder." He stretched out a hand toward Leeuwenhoek. "You . . . you knew Julie. You knew her very well. She was the woman who trampled on your deepest feelings . . . who played with you . . . who misled you . . . who forced a child upon you that wasn't yours. If anybody had a motive to kill Black Julie, it was you." He paced a few times up and down in front of DeKok's desk and then leaned over the visitor. "But you, Charles Leeuwenhoek, you were not present at the seance. You cannot be the murderer, not the *actual* murderer. You had no opportunity to put the poison in her coffee." Vledder grinned falsely. "But then, you didn't have to do it yourself, did you? You have a sister . . . a sister who has supported you all her life . . . a resourceful and decisive sister, who in the past . . . and now . . . was not afraid to commit murder."

Charles Leeuwenhoek hid his face in his hands and seemed to shrink where he sat. The words affected him like whip lashes. Fiercely he shook his head.

"It isn't true," he cried out. "It isn't true." He gave DeKok a supplicating look. "Make him stop. Please . . . make him, stop. Annette didn't do it. Annette . . ." He was unable to go on. He took several deep breaths, tried to control himself. A look of wonder came into his eyes, a hint of doubt. "And if . . . if Annette *did* do it, I didn't want it, I wouldn't have wanted her to do it. Not me. I loved Julie. Believe me, I loved her. Even if she had given me ten illegitimate children . . . I could have cared less . . . as long as she didn't leave me . . . if she had only wanted to stay with me."

* * *

There was a derisive smile on DeKok's face.

"Well, you certainly were in top form," he mocked. "You almost had poor Charles confess to a murder he couldn't possibly have committed."

Vledder shook his head with irritation.

"I just couldn't keep it in any longer. In any case, by now it's pretty clear that Annette lays down the law in the Leeuwenhoek family. If she hadn't interfered, Julie and Charles would maybe still have been a happy couple."

DeKok grinned wickedly.

"Including a red-haired child by Klaver."

Vledder snorted.

"But no matter what, he seemed to accept the possibility that his sister *had* killed Black Julie. Apparently he judged her to be capable of doing just that. Remember what he said: '... if Annette *did* do it, I didn't want it ...' That sounds pretty conclusive to me."

DeKok shrugged.

"It doesn't mean much to me," he said carelessly. "It seems the typical expression of a man who consistently has shirked responsibility... passed the buck, so to speak. I have an idea that Annette, as older sister, often had to make his decisions for him."

There was determined look on Vledder's face.

"Whatever," he said, "if there *were* murder attempts on Julie's life in the past, then it had to be the work of Annette ... not Charles. I'm sure of that, by now. I'm beginning to think that Annette is indeed a devilish woman. As far as I'm concerned, she also killed her first husband."

DeKok laughed out loud.

"Better watch out, that lady can cause us a lot of trouble."

"How?"

DeKok pulled his lower lip and let it plop back. It was one of his more annoying habits. Vledder stared at him angrily while DeKok repeated the gesture several times.

"Well," urged Vledder, exasperated.

"Well," said DeKok, "what do you think dear brother is doing right now? I bet you that he went straight to his older sister to complain about the outrageous behavior of that young Inspector at Warmoes Street, the one who uttered such chilling accusations."

Vledder's mouth fell open.

"You're right," he said finally. He sighed. "Tactically it was a disaster. Annette has now been warned. She knows what we suspect. Perhaps I should have waited with my accusations until we interrogate her in person."

DeKok smiled benignly.

"Sometimes, Dick Vledder, you make intelligent remarks." He paused. "By the way," he added, "did you notice that Charles referred to his wife as Julie, not Jane?"

7

There was a mild sun and the flags around the piers for the sightseeing boats waved gaily against a stark blue sky. His hat far back on his head, his hands deep in the pockets of his raincoat, DeKok ambled leisurely along the wide sidewalk of the Damrak. The strange murder in seance kept him occupied. He hoped that the new day would smile upon him. Detective work was, after all, a matter of knowledge, experience, insight and above all, luck. He hoped that Lady Luck would be well disposed toward him and would give him just a little bit of a break. The longer an investigation lingered, the smaller the chances of success. He looked around and was pleased with what he saw.

The number of women and girls that had taken advantage of the warm sun seemed to have doubled and to DeKok they were all beautiful. He stopped near Old Bridge Alley and looked at the sightseeing boats. Long rows of tourists were patiently awaiting their turn to board, while large crowds of tourists were being discharged from the boats that had just returned. It was a festive and peaceful sight. Come and see Amsterdam, he thought. And why not? Amsterdam was a beautiful city . . . even if somebody, from time to time, was killed in a very unpleasant way.

An extremely attractive woman in tight pants passed by, her hips gently swaying in a most enticing manner. He stood and watched her for several seconds before he turned with a sigh and disappeared in the direction of the station house.

* * *

DeKok waved at Vledder from behind his desk, putting away a bag of licorice from which he had just made a selection.

"How was the autopsy?" asked DeKok when Vledder had come closer.

The young Inspector stopped in front of the desk and grimaced.

"You may not believe it, but Dr. Rusteloos was extremely interested in our investigation. He asked to be kept informed of our progress."

DeKok looked up, surprise on his face.

"But why?"

"He said that he was not very familiar with cases of poisoning by hydrocyanic acid and he was interested to know how the poison had been obtained and how it had been administered. He had encountered suicide, he said, where the substance was used and also been involved with some industrial accidents where people were killed as the result of hydrocyanic acid, but he had never encountered it as a murder weapon."

DeKok looked thoughtful.

"Did he say industrial accidents?"

Vledder nodded emphatically.

"According to Dr. Rusteloos there are many industries where hydrocyanic acid is used regularly. In the chemical industry, for instance, and also in the photographic industry. Also, hydrocyanic acid is used a lot for fighting pests. In most agricultural concerns there is enough hydrocyanic acid present to wipe out entire communities."

DeKok snorted.

"Well, from that I understand that it isn't all that difficult to get hold of the stuff."

Vledder nodded.

"As with many poisons, it's easy to get . . . in bulk."

DeKok rubbed the bridge of his nose with a little finger. There was a regretful look on his face as he swallowed the last of his licorice. He opened the drawer of his desk and looked at the almost full bag of sweets. Then, with a resolute gesture he closed the drawer again.

"We can safely assume," he said somberly, "that Jane died because of hydrocyanic acid, or Prussic acid."

Vledder leaned on the desk.

"It's practically a certainty. The pathologist pointed out the extremely clear color of the post mortem lividity. He also thought that hydrocyanic acid poisoning would be easily established during the toxicological investigation. In any case, he gave me quite a load of samples to take over. Parts of the body, urine, stomach and intestine contents, stuff like that."

DeKok smiled.

"Did the good doctor say anything about the antabuse effect?"

"Antabuse? Isn't that a trademark, or something?"

"Yes, for a drug to cure alcoholism, or rather when taking Antabuse, alcohol has a bad taste and tends to make you sick. But in this case I'm not speaking about the specific drug, although the name has been well chosen. Antabuse effect describes the intensified action of a particular poison in combination with another."

Vledder shrugged, silently amazed at DeKok's encyclopedic knowledge of obscure facts.

"He did ask if Jane had been using any drugs or stimulants."

DeKok nodded into the distance.

"I expected that, more or less. I've been asking the same question myself. The pupils were strongly dilated. I have seen that sort of widening with older women who use *bella donna* to make their eyes shine brighter."

Vledder laughed.

"Is that why they call it *bella donna*?"

"It's a bit out of fashion, although it is still frequently used in Homeopathic Medicine. But these days stronger remedies are used. Perhaps Gerard Klaver can tell us what Black Julie used. But personally, I don't believe in it. I suspect that the murderer added a stimulating ingredient to the hydrocyanic acid."

Vledder sank into the chair behind his own desk, scant inches from DeKok's desk.

"To make sure the effect would be fatal?"

DeKok shook his head.

"Out of pity."

Vledder looked astonished.

"Out of pity?"

DeKok nodded gravely.

"To make sure that death would be as near instantaneous as possible, you understand? Even faster than with just hydrocyanic acid. To curtail the suffering of the victim as much as possible."

Vledder licked dry lips.

"That . . . eh," he hesitated, "would indicate some sort of relationship, kinship . . . affinity."

DeKok's face was expressionless.

"Perhaps," he answered softly, "perhaps even love."

* * *

Aad Ishoven, the chief of administration at Warmoes Street station, tossed a file on DeKok's desk. Dust flew in every direction as the file connected with the desk top. The gray sleuth stared at it, an annoyed look on his face. Then he glanced up.

"What's the meaning of this?"

Aad Ishoven stared back at DeKok for several seconds. There was confusion behind his glasses.

"But didn't you ask for this? It's the file on Martin Stekel."

"Who is that?"

Aad pointed at the gray, dust covered folder.

"Just read it . . . I'm sure you'll find what you're looking for." He sputtered to himself. "And it took me more than an hour to find it, too." He turned around and walked away. "That's gratitude for you," he was heard to say.

Vledder pulled the file toward him.

"It's the investigation of twelve years ago," he said after a few seconds. "In regard to the rumors that Martin Stekel had not died a natural death, but supposedly was gradually poisoned."

DeKok gripped his head with both hands.

"Of course . . . the late husband of Annette Leeuwenhoek." Then a look of amazement came over him. "So . . . there *was* an investigation, after all."

Vledder slapped the file and another dust cloud rose in the air.

"This is it," he said simply. "And from what I've seen so far, it was a thorough investigation."

DeKok sighed elaborately. Then he opened the drawer of his desk and grabbed a handful of licorice. Thoughtfully he chewed while Vledder waited patiently as DeKok satisfied his sweet tooth.

"You should read the file," advised DeKok finally. "Perhaps there's something in it we can use. Look up the final conclusion."

Vledder smiled. DeKok's aversion to reading, and writing, reports was well known. He picked up the file and after a little search, pulled out a single sheet.

"Let's see," said Vledder. "Here it is: ... after an exhaustive investigation it was impossible to prove that Martin Stekel died other than a natural death ... it was equally impossible to prove, or to establish any basis in fact to the rumors that Martin Stekel had been poisoned by his wife, Annette Leeuwenhoek."

DeKok grinned smugly.

"Very nice. You could have written that."

"What do you mean?"

"They could have just written that Martin wasn't poisoned and his wife didn't do it. I mean, really, ... impossible to prove ... other than natural death ..."

Vledder shook his head.

"The report was written by Inspector Bierdrager, now long since retired."

DeKok rubbed his chin.

"But the rumors about the poisoning have been persistent," he said seriously. "Even after twelve years they have not disappeared."

Vledder nodded to himself, contemplating what portion of the dusty file should be transferred to his computer.

"Yes, the poisoning of Jane Truffle has brought those old rumors once again to the fore. It's about time we go see old auntie Leeuwenhoek and ask her some questions."

"That won't be necessary," said a husky voice. "I'm here."

Vledder and DeKok looked up in surprise. They had been so engrossed in their discussion that they had not noticed the approach of a woman. They saw a striking figure, tall, big and a bit tawny. She wore boots that reached to below her knees and a long, flowing, brown cape over a linen blouse and a long skirt.

She rubbed gray hair from her face and looked pointedly at the chair next to DeKok's desk.

"I regret not having myself properly announced," she said cynically, "but one of the . . . eh, gentlemen near the door pointed out your desk." She turned toward Vledder. "I didn't mean to eavesdrop, but I heard part of what you said and I would like to point out that there's no question of there being any possible family relationship between me and . . . you. In other words, I'm *not* your auntie."

Vledder had the grace to blush.

"It . . . eh, it was more a form of speech," he tried to apologize. "In Amsterdam vernacular the expression 'auntie' covers a number of situations."

She turned abruptly away, threw her cape over one shoulder and sat down on the chair next to DeKok's desk.

"Please sit down," said DeKok belatedly, as he stood up. His usual, suave courtesy had been found wanting with the sudden appearance of this formidable old lady.

"I was the subject of your deliberations?" she asked tartly, ignoring both DeKok's invitation and the fact that he had stood up. She addressed the space that would have been occupied by his head, if he had still been seated.

DeKok sat down and gave her a winning smile. He leaned back in his chair and made an affirmative gesture.

"Indeed," he said, "you did . . . and have, our undivided attention."

She plucked at the sleeve of her worsted linen blouse.

"And I'm supposed to be happy with that?"

DeKok shrugged slightly, maintaining his smile.

"We, policemen, are strange creatures. We're always looking for proof." He paused, looked at her. "Proof of guilt, proof of innocence. The death of your sister-in-law, Jane Truffle, has brought a number of things to the surface." He pointed at the dusty file on Vledder's desk. "It has opened old wounds."

Annette Leeuwenhoek nodded resolutely.

"That old affair with my first husband. It caused me a lot of grief and misery at the time. In retrospect Martin Stekel was a . . . eh, a peculiar person. Much different from when we were engaged. He turned out to be jealous, suspicious, possessive . . . almost sickly." She shook her head. "Our marriage was not what I had dreamed it to be. Very early on there were tensions . . . perhaps also because I was rather independent, right from the start. Martin always complained to everybody who would listen. According to him the failure of our marriage wasn't his fault, but mine. He accused me of not taking care of him, neglecting the household for secret love affairs and so on. There was no ground for his accusations, but in the end I stopped trying to defend myself. He also accused me of attempting to poison him. It was just another of his idiotic statements. Fortunately, nobody believed him." She sighed deeply and again rubbed the hair from her face. "When nobody paid enough attention, he started to fake suicides."

DeKok gave her a searching look.

"Fake?"

Annette looked discouraged, as if she had told the story many times and just as often had not been believed.

"He set the stage. For instance, he would take too many sleeping pills and then make sure he would be discovered in time. He would cut his wrists, but was careful not to severe any arteries. You understand? The attempts were not for real. They were aimed at creating a feeling of guilt in me." Her voice suddenly changed, instead of the husky undertone, it became sharp and forceful. "But I did not feel guilty. I had nothing to feel guilty about. I mean, it wasn't I that made his life impossible. It was just a delusion, an *idee fixe*. It wasn't until much later that I learned there had been mental aberrations in his family for some time."

"But he died a natural death?"

She nodded slowly, absent-mindedly.

"He died of what was then called *manager's disease.* Today, I understand, they call it *stress.* In any case, a heart disease as the result of excessive physical and mental exertions. It happened rather suddenly and nobody had expected it. Martin was still young, barely thirty-seven." She paused, rubbed some stray hair from her forehead. "And then the gossip started. I never did find out who started it. The first time I heard something, was a few days after Martin's funeral. A friend told me. She said that it was whispered that I had poisoned Martin. At first I shrugged it off, tried to ignore it, but then . . . one day the police were at my door."

"Inspector Bierdrager."

A wan smile played around her thin lips.

"A friendly man. Truly. I can only praise the way in which he performed his tasks. Very discreet and accommodating. Later he told me that his investigations did not uncover any damaging evidence against me and that he would say so in his report. He was unable to establish any crime in connection with the death of my husband."

DeKok nodded.

"We read Inspector Bierdrager's conclusion," he said. "There was no exhumation?"

Annette Leeuwenhoek sighed deeply.

"At least I've been spared *that* shame. According to the Inspector, the Judge-Advocate could not find any compelling reasons for an exhumation."

"The investigation was shortly after the funeral?"

She made an apologetic gesture.

"I can't be expected to know how long the Inspector was digging around before he contacted me. The only thing I know for sure, is that the investigation was closed about three months after my husband died." She lowered her head. There was a sad smile on her face when she looked up again. "You would have expected that after the police investigation, the gossip would stop, wouldn't you? But that didn't happen. It lingered and lingered. Sometimes I wouldn't hear anything for a year and then it would start all over again."

DeKok looked at her evenly.

"Such as now?"

"Exactly . . . like now. I know what people say about me. I am supposed to be responsible for Jane's death. Apparently I put something in her coffee during the seance." She made a helpless gesture. "What can I say? It's just as ridiculous as that I should have killed my first husband."

Vledder leaned closer.

"According to remarks made by your sister-in-law, there have been attempts on her life in the past."

Annette Leeuwenhoek turned toward Vledder, a pitying look on her face.

"And you believe that?"

Vledder shrugged.

"I simply repeat what I've heard others say."

She shook her head. For a moment DeKok expected her to wag a finger at Vledder.

"My dear Inspector," she said denigratingly, "surely you're smarter than that? Who is . . . or was Jane Truffle . . . more commonly known as Black Julie? You must be familiar with that type of woman? Not to be trusted and with a rampant imagination. In her best years Julie was . . . how shall I put it . . . a not unattractive, frivolous girl of easy morals. Did you know she waited tables without a stitch on? Anyway, I'll try to be as delicate as possible. Her only redeeming quality, if you can call it that, is that she managed to make my poor brother fall in love with her and then pressed him into an undesirable marriage."

Vledder stretched out a hand toward her.

"And you opposed the marriage?"

She gave him a look as if he were something found under a rock.

"Of course I was against the marriage. That marriage *had* to fail. It was obvious that she only married to give the child she carried the Leeuwenhoek name . . . including all the financial benefits adherent thereto."

"And still are."

She moved her head up and down.

"Yes, agreed, he's still entitled to the rewards. Richard is still . . . God knows if the child is still alive . . . but he is still the son of Charles . . . legally." A blush appeared on her cheeks. "Murder attempts," she exclaimed suddenly. "*she* talked about murder attempts?" There was disgust and indignation in her voice. "Do you know that she conceived a devilish plan to kill Charles?"

"Who? Julie?"

Annette Leeuwenhoek snorted. Her nostrils quivered with anger.

"One night, when Charles was a bit under the weather . . . not to put too fine a point on it . . . he had drunk a little too much. Anyway, that night she drove them both home, parked the car in the garage, closed the doors and left Charles in the car with the engine running. For some reason the engine conked out and they were barely able to save Charles. When Charles was confronted with the facts . . . yes, yes, at my urging, he sent Black Julie *and* her red-haired child away . . . showed them the door, he did." She paused, took a deep breath and calmed down a little. "Charles is a lummox. He should have taken immediate steps, at that time.

Our lawyers were convinced that Julie, considering the circumstances, would be more than ready to agree to a divorce under advantageous terms." She closed her eyes. "But Charles refused. On the contrary, if he had had his way, he would have gone to her on his knees and he would have begged her to come back to him."

"He never married again?"

She shook her head.

"Impossible. As soon as Black Julie understood that she had nothing to fear from Charles, she resisted every attempt at a divorce."

Vledder grinned.

"And even threats didn't change her mind?"

Annette reacted fiercely.

"She was never threatened . . . not by us."

DeKok stood up and walked over to the coffee machine.

"Would you like some coffee?" he asked in a friendly voice.

She looked at him, suspicion in her eyes.

"Black, a little sugar."

8

DeKok gave Vledder a worried look.

"I'm sorry but I can't help it," he said, shaking his head, "but whenever poison comes into the picture, I always have the feeling we're just seeing the tip of the iceberg."

"What do you mean?" asked Vledder.

DeKok made a tired gesture.

"As far as I'm concerned, there are a lot more murders by poison in our country than the few that come to the notice of the police."

Vledder smiled.

"What brought that on?"

"Do you remember the case of the poisoned student? Delzen?"

"Oh, yes. I remember. What about it."*

"At that time I had a long conversation with Dr. Eskes. He said that the number of *attempted* poisonings happens to be rather high. 'You would be amazed if you knew how many times a person attempts to poison another. And not only in the Netherlands. It is the same all over the world, wherever such statistics are maintained,' said Dr. Eskes. He went on to say that

* See: *DeKok and the Dying Stroller.*

an *attempted* poisoning is a murder that did not succeed. He said: 'It is discovered in time. And how is it discovered? In other words . . . what is the origin of the discovery. Well, the potential victim does not feel well and visits a doctor. In some cases the victim will mention the possibility of poisoning, in other cases an alert physician may observe the symptoms. People may speak of *food poisoning*, or say they ate something *that did not agree with them*. Whatever the reason, it is always the victim who sets in motion the chain of events that will, eventually, lead to a criminal investigation.' Then he asked: 'But what happens if the victim is no longer able to communicate? In other words, if the attempted poisoning was successful?' And he answered his own question with: 'Then, my dear friend, nobody knows, not even the famous DeKok.'"

"Really?" commented Vledder, who had no doubt that DeKok had just reported the entire conversation verbatim.

"Really," affirmed DeKok, pulling open a drawer of his desk. He pushed away an assortment of various candy bars and pulled out several sheets, paper clipped together, and covered with graphs. Before he closed the drawer he made a selection from among the confections and happily unwrapped a bar of chocolate. He pushed shut the drawer and showed the graphs to Vledder.

"I went to the trouble of checking Dr. Eskes' assertions," he said with a mouth full of chocolate. He swallowed and then added: "And Dr. Eskes was right. There are many more attempts at murder than murders."

"So?"

"And that should not be possible," answered DeKok, irritation in his voice. "The difference is too lop-sided. For instance, two murders and more than a hundred attempts. That's not right. There should be more corpses."

"Why?"

DeKok placed his hands flat on the desk.

"Dr. Eskes provided the answer. If a person doesn't complain about feeling unwell, or about having eaten something disagreeable . . . but simply dies? You see what I mean?"

"Yes, of course. The victim is simply buried and nobody's the wiser."

DeKok gave him a satisfied smile.

"Exactly . . . nobody's the wiser." He raised a finger in the air. "Also, please keep in mind that there's always premeditation when poison is used . . . calm, cool, planning . . . a cunning murderer, or murderess, if there is such a word."

Vledder swallowed.

"Would Annette Leeuwenhoek . . .?" He hesitated. "She certainly strikes me as cunning and determined enough."

DeKok did not answer at once.

"I must presume," he said finally, "that our colleague, Bierdrager, performed a thorough investigation. It would be useless to start looking for new clues after all this time. And if Annette used cyanide, or a cyanide derivative at that time, exhumation would be useless as well. Cyanide dissipates within six months or so. Only if something like *thallium* or arsenic has been used would we have a chance. Thallium and arsenic are heavy metals and remain detectable for a long period of time. If large doses have been administered, over an extended period of time, they can actually act as a preservative. The bodies remain intact longer. A modified mummification process, so to speak."

Vledder thought he had a point to make.

"But you can't be sure," he said.

"You mean whether or not Annette used thallium, or arsenic, at the time?"

"Yes."

DeKok shook his head.

"Most poisoners have the tendency to stick with a particular poison . . . especially if it has been used successfully." He looked up. "Do you have the list of all the women who were present at the seance?"

Vledder nodded. With one hand he pulled out his notebook and with the other he brought the necessary information onto the screen of his computer.

"Jennifer Jordan," he read out.

DeKok shook his head.

"The medium. And she's blind. I believe she's the only one we can safely scratch off as a suspect."

"Unless she had an accomplice."

DeKok pursed his lips.

"A possibility," he admitted after a moment's thought. "Not a bad idea." There was praise in his voice. "For instance, Christine Vanwal, her friend . . . with, or without, the cooperation of Harry Donkers, the nephew. But we're left with the problem of a motive." He rubbed his chin. "Who else have we got?"

"Agatha Cologne."

DeKok laughed, a bit bitter. In his mind's eye he saw the old, fierce, wrinkled face under the frivolous straw hat.

"A woman," he commented, "with enough venom in her soul to be capable of a poisoning."

Vledder ignored the remark.

"Next on the list is Mathilda Lochem, the sister of our esteemed Judge-Advocate."

DeKok stared into the distance.

"I can't make up my mind about her," he said with a sigh. "We haven't had a chance to talk to her in detail. She seems to be type of woman who spies from behind the curtains on what the neighbors are doing."

Vledder compared the entries in his notebook with the list on the screen.

"Then there is Josephine Dahlmeyer, fifty-two and the wife of a stock broker. Very rich, according to reports. Finally Irene Peters, wife of an extremely absent-minded professor in biology."

"Biology?"

"Yes, biology . . . something the matter with that?"

"Maybe," sighed DeKok. "She could have picked up some knowledge of toxicology from her husband. For instance, the use and application of certain garden and agricultural poisons."

"Cyanide is used in green houses."

"Exactly. Who else?"

"Marie Vaart. A member of the circle for years. Fifty-three and married to a writer of detective stories."

DeKok grinned.

"We must definitely talk to that couple. Perhaps her husband can teach us a thing or two."

Vledder nodded without enthusiasm.

"Next is Babette Vanson. Unmarried and a close friend of Agatha Cologne. Agatha took her to the seance to take the place of her late sister, Martha." Vledder paused. "And that leaves only one more."

"Who?"

"Annette Leeuwenhoek . . . I'm betting on her."

DeKok gave him an indulgent look. He pushed the graphs back in his drawer, looked at his watch and stood up.

"It's already past eight. Tonight there's nothing left to do for us. All those involved have gathered for tonight's seance."

Vledder smirked.

"Including our distinguished Commissaris and the Judge-Advocate."

DeKok shook his head sadly.

"In an attempt to learn the identity of a living killer from the spirits of the dead." he sighed deeply. "It would be laughable if it wasn't so very, very sad." He walked over to the coat rack. "I have a better idea."

Vledder laughed out loud.

"I know and it's called Little Lowee's."

DeKok joined in the laughter.

"Well done. Good guess."

* * *

Dressed in his raincoat, the belt like a rope around his middle, DeKok ambled through the heart of his beloved Amsterdam and looked at the people around him. He liked to look at people as they were a constant source of interest to him. All people are unique and no matter how despicable, each was a different creature from the next.

DeKok ignored the explicit posters outside the sex theaters and he wasted not a glance at the abundance of dildoes in the sex boutiques. He was of the opinion that sex was something to be done, to experience, not something to be looked at. Sex did not need artificial stimulation, certainly not mass-produced, factory products. Besides, he admitted to himself, despite his long career in and around the Red Light District, his puritanical soul still objected to the shameless exhibition of one of mankind's most intimate moments. Even a dyed-in-the-wool prostitute, he mused, had the decency to close the curtains when she was with a client. Prostitutes were another matter entirely, in DeKok's mind. According to him they served a useful function in society by allowing the sex-starved, or those who thought they were, an acceptable and safe outlet, thus protecting the general population. Not for the first time, DeKok reflected that he was too complicated a personality for his own good.

Vledder tapped him on the shoulder and drew his attention toward a pickpocket, who had his eyes on a purse, dangling carelessly from the arm of a woman. When the woman and her companion entered a bar, the pickpocket turned away, a disappointed look on his face. With a start he recognized DeKok, who shook his head with disapproval. The pickpocket shrugged, grinned shyly, knuckled his forehead and disappeared in the crowd.

Vledder and DeKok proceeded apace. Occasionally DeKok would return the greeting of one of the denizens of the Quarter and every once in a while he stopped to exchange a few words. Through all this, Vledder was studiously ignored by the regulars. Vledder, after all, was a cop, but DeKok was part of their environment.

At the corner of Barn Alley, they entered the quiet, cozy bar of Little Lowee.

* * *

A tall man is sometimes called "Tiny" and a slow person may be referred to as "Speedy". But Lowee was called "Little," because he *was* small. His real name was probably Louis, something or other. Only his mother and DeKok probably knew the real name. Throughout the Red Light District and throughout a large part of the Amsterdam underworld he had always been known as Little Lowee.

The diminutive barkeeper showed a broad grin when Vledder and DeKok entered.

"Good day," he chirped, "Well come." His mousy face was a picture of happiness. Since time immemorial he had always considered DeKok as a particular friend. "I just done finished the obits but you wasn't in it."

DeKok looked askance.

"You thought I was dead?"

Little Lowee winked.

"Well," he said indignantly, "you ain't been by for a long time." He almost pouted when he added: "And there's such a lotta them clowns with heaters nowadays, you never knows, you don't. I's *that* worried sometimes."

DeKok was touched.

"Worried about me?"

The barkeeper made a vague gesture.

"Well, I's a businessman, you knows. I wanna keep me customers." With a quick movement he lowered himself below the level of the bar and resurfaced with a fine bottle of cognac. He held it with pride as he showed the label to DeKok. "Whadda you think of this, then. Not bad, eh? I don't wanna see it go to waste, you knows."

DeKok closed his eyes in anticipated delight.

"Lowee," he said with sincere admiration, "you're a wonder. Your loyalty and your good taste exceed all expectations."

The barkeeper placed three large snifters on the bar and with reverent movements removed the cork. Then he poured generous measures in the waiting glasses.

DeKok lifted his glass, rocked it slightly in his hand and inhaled the aroma. There was a look of utter delight on his face as he savored the fragrance. Carefully he raised the glass in a silent toast and took a sip. He closed his eyes as the amber liquid warmed his innards.

"You know, Lowee," he said dreamily, "there are moments in life that I can reconcile myself to being a cop."

Vledder and Lowee laughed politely and took a sip themselves.

"Excellent," commented Vledder.

Lowee ignored him. His regard for DeKok did not extend to engaging in conversation with DeKok's apprentice, as he usually referred to Vledder.

DeKok silently enjoyed his drink. Cognac was more than just a drink to DeKok. It was almost a sacrament, something to be savored with total attention and he especially liked these quiet moments in Lowee's bar, where he had been a regular visitor since the time he was still a uniformed constable. With a tender, almost devout gesture, he placed the empty glass on the bar.

"Pour once more, my friend," he urged.

Lowee was obviously flattered by the way he was addressed and he obeyed with alacrity.

"How's things atta station?"

"A madhouse," growled DeKok, watching him pour.

"You gotta do somethin' with the stiff from them spooks?"

"What spooks?"

"You knows, them dames that talk to spooks."

"What do you know about it?"

"Well, them dames called onna bunch of spooks and one came outta nowheres and kills Black Julie."

"You knew Black Julie?"

Lowee nodded.

"Sure I knows her. I knowed her when she still ran around nekkid inna whorehouse over at Thorbecke Square. She were no more than sixteen, seventeen atta time, I thinks." He saw the beginning of a frown on DeKok's face. "Hey, hey," he added quickly, "she don't do no tricks, you knows, just waited tables anna . . . she do, *done* look a lot older than she were, you knows." He gestured. "Later she usta hang around here a lot, before they called on them spooks."

"Spirits," corrected Vledder.

Lowee could not let that pass.

"I got spirits," he said with dignity, "them dames call on spooks."

DeKok lifted his glass and took a sip.

"Any idea why they would want to kill her?" he asked casually.

Lowee shook his head sadly.

"I don't. Ain't heard a thing until after. Everybody think itsa crazy thing to happen. Some of the guys tell me there's crazy things happening in that there house, anyways."

DeKok looked at him, translating Lowee's Amsterdam slang in his mind.

"What sort of strange happenings?"

"Well, with them dead spooks, or . . . ghosts," he corrected with a triumphant look in Vledder's direction. "They done tell me they make a table dance and what not."

DeKok smiled.

"That's a lot different from murder."

Little Lowee looked around the almost empty bar and then leaned closer.

"You knows she's stinking rich, don't ye?" he asked in a hoarse whisper.

"Who?"

"The dame . . . the blind dame that calls the sp . . . *ghosts*."

"Jennifer Jordan"

Little Lowee looked serious.

"Yep, that's her moniker, alright. She done inher . . . inher . . . her father left her lotsa moolah when he croaked. Paintings, jewels, stamps. Her old man was some high muckedymuck from Limey Land. A Lord or somethin', who done married a Dutch broad."

"Jennifer's mother."

"Yep, exactum, I tole you. I never knowed the mother. I knowed Jennifer, all right. I knowed 'er when she wasn't blind."

He paused, sipped his cognac. "We done made some plans atta time."

"Who?"

"Me and some of them guys."

"What kind of plans?"

Lowee shrugged his shoulders, a reluctant look on his face.

"Well, you knows, to take a look in her house, you knows. When she weren't there, of course."

"Burglary."

The barkeeper grimaced.

"You use all them nasty words." He took another sip. "No, not *burglary*, just, you knows, take a look . . . just to see iffen it was worth it."

"Case the joint," remarked Vledder. Lowee pretended not to hear. He stared into the distance.

"But that never happened?" asked DeKok.

Little Lowee shook his head.

"Nah, before we coulda done somethin' about it, we hear she's gone blind."

"So you cancelled the plans."

Lowee gave him a sad look.

"You don't steal from no blind person, you just don't."

DeKok smiled and lifted his glass.

"You're absolutely right, Lowee . . . I agree . . . you don't steal from a blind person."

* * *

It was already late when DeKok and Vledder finally left Lowee's intimate little bar. It drizzled again, but the business in the District continued unabated. Slowly the prospective customers and the tourists moved from one lighted window to the next, staring at the often exotically beautiful women who displayed themselves in various stages of undress. One of them tapped on the window as the two Inspectors passed by. They looked up and saw an extremely good looking blonde prostitute, dressed in a revealing, lace bodysuit, wave at them. Vledder blushed, but DeKok merely gave a friendly wave in return.

"They call her BB," said DeKok, "Because she looks like Brigitte Bardot."

"Why did she wave at us?"

"I arrested her pimp a few months ago and chased him out of town. She's on her own now and apparently a lot happier."

"When did you do that?" asked Vledder, curious.

"As I said, a few months ago."

"I didn't know about it."

"It was of no importance. I just asked him to come to the station with me and then I had a conversation. After that he thought it advisable to move to Rotterdam, or Antwerp . . . I don't know."

"What about the girl?"

"As I said, she's now on her own, keeping all the money she makes. She's enrolled at the university, studying to be a doctor."

Vledder digested that information. The more he knew about DeKok, the more he realized that there were unknown depths to his old partner. Only in Holland could a prostitute receive protection from the police, study to be a doctor and have some reasonable hope of a successful medical career.

DeKok pushed his hat forward and glanced at Vledder.

"It's late already. Go home, tomorrow is another day."

"What about you?"

DeKok smiled.

"I'll just look in at the office and then I'll go home too. There are complaints about my marital fidelity."

Vledder waved and disappeared in the crowd. With his hands deep in the pockets of his raincoat, DeKok continued toward Warmoes Street. Now that he was outside, ever since they left Lowee's bar, he had felt a vague sense of depression. He had the feeling that something had happened. He nodded at a few constables as he entered the station house. Meindert Post looked up from his place behind the desk, a grin on his face.

"Your boss," he said mockingly, "is doing better than you."

"What are you talking about?"

Meindert Post gave him a smug nod.

"Yessir, the Commissaris and the Judge-Advocate have arrested your murderer. He's in the cells, downstairs."

"What murderer?"

Post grinned broadly.

"Black Julie's murderer."

9

With a face like a thundercloud DeKok entered the office of Commissaris Buitendam. He was highly upset. He did not like it when others meddled with his investigations and always resisted any such interference forcefully. The fact that his own chief, aided and abetted by the Judge-Advocate, had possessed the temerity to make an arrest in a case he considered his own, made the transgression worse in his eyes. Wide, angry and immovable he stopped in front of the desk.

"You wanted to see me?" asked DeKok in measured tones.

There was a smug, challenging smile on the commissarial face as he looked up at his subordinate.

"Yes, indeed, DeKok," he said in his cultured, affected voice. "I think the time has come to go over that murder in the canal house together." He pointed at a chair. "Please have a seat."

"I'd rather stand," said DeKok grumpily.

The Commissaris worried with his necktie.

"As you wish, DeKok." He coughed. "It seems to me that that particular murder is as good as solved."

DeKok's face was expressionless.

"Congratulations."

The Commissaris leaned back in his chair, brought the tips of his long, pointed fingers together and smiled benignly.

"Yes. It was an inspired suggestion of Mathilda . . . eh, I mean Ms. Lochem. The spiritualistic seance she arranged for the Judge-Advocate and myself turned out to be a resounding success. I must say. The medium, Mrs. Jordan, is extremely sensitive and she almost immediately contacted the spirit world. Impressive. The second manifestation already indicated Donkers as the perpetrator."

DeKok's eyes narrowed.

"Harry Donkers?"

Buitendam nodded agreeably.

"Exactly, correct, yes. The nephew of the medium, of Mrs. Jordan. We immediately proceeded with the arrest last night."

DeKok cocked his head at his chief.

"On the basis of the statement of eh, . . . of a ghost?"

The Commissaris shook his head.

"Not just that. It was a point of departure, no more. After the announcement we knew where to direct our attention."

DeKok grinned disbelievingly.

"At Harry Donkers?"

The Commissaris nodded again, a smug look on his face.

"Yes, some surprising facts came to light after that. After we interrogated all the women present, we came to the conclusion that Donkers could have been the only one to add poison to the coffee that day."

"And then you arrested him?"

"Yes."

"Has he confessed?"

The Commissaris did not answer at once. He picked up a fountain pen from his desk and twirled it between his fingers.

"The man denies all knowledge," he said finally, hesitatingly. "Both the Judge-Advocate and myself are of the opinion that he will have to be interrogated thoroughly." He replaced the pen on the desk and looked up at DeKok. "We felt it best that *you* do the interrogation. There's no denying the fact that you have a lot of experience in these matters."

DeKok took a deep breath, trying to control the anger he felt rising inside himself. He felt his blood run faster and knew his face was getting red. The tips of fingers itched and he wanted to scream that both the Commissaris and the Judge-Advocate could jump in the lake and that he didn't have the slightest intention of interrogating Harry Donkers. With an effort he controlled himself. He balled his hands into fists and pressed the nails of his fingers deep into his palms. He shuddered and swallowed several times. The Commissaris looked expectantly from across the desk.

"I," said DeKok between clenched teeth, "will do the interrogation."

A relieved smile showed on the commissarial face.

"Very good, DeKok," he said. "That's a load off my mind. I know he's in good hands."

DeKok bit his lower lip until he thought the blood would spurt out.

"Do you have any witnesses?" he asked.

"What sort of witnesses" asked Buitendam, surprised.

"People who witnessed that Harry Donkers put poison in the coffee."

Commissaris Buitendam laughed and waved his hand in the air.

"Of course not, DeKok. The guy is smart. What did you expect? No, he's very smart, that's evident from everything. He did not participate in the seance, as usual. While the others were fully occupied with the medium and what was happening during the seance, he was completely undisturbed as he executed his nefarious plans." He paused and coughed for effect. "Frankly, both the Judge-Advocate and myself were a bit surprised that you and Vledder did not arrest him at once, while you were at the scene."

DeKok rubbed the bridge of his nose with a little finger. He was again able to see the humor of the situation.

"Well, we lacked the information from a helpful ghost," said DeKok sarcastically.

Buitendam gave him a thoughtful look, wondering whether or not he had been mocked.

"It might be well," said the Commissaris in a didactic tone, "if you concentrated a bit more on learning about transcendental matters. It could very well be vital to the development of this case. Personally, I'm convinced that we are receiving messages from the hereafter. We must open ourselves up to them."

DeKok snorted. The condescending tone of the Commissaris was too much for his barely controlled anger. With a resigned sigh he felt himself nearing the edge.

"What those people in that canal house do," he said in a loud voice, "is their business. But if they start to kill off each other, I'll do something about it . . . in my own way." He took a deep breath. "There has *never* been a single murder solved by a medium . . . no matter how sensitive. And if the press gets a hold of the grounds for Harry's arrest, I fear the worst for your career . . . and that of the Judge-Advocate."

Buitendam stood up, angry blushes on his cheeks. With a shaking hand he pointed at the door.

"OUT!"

DeKok left.

* * *

DeKok flopped down in the chair behind his desk. His face was gray and the lines around his mouth seemed deeper. The recent conversation with Buitendam had affected him more than he cared to admit. Often, almost always, he had been of a different opinion than his Chief when handling a case and the ensuing conversations generally resulted in bitter recriminations, or a shouting match. But in the end the Commissaris had always allowed him to go his own way, never before had he personally interfered. He took a deep breath and banished his anger.

"They arrested Harry Donkers last night," he said wanly.

Vledder looked up with interest.

"Who?"

"The Commissaris and the Judge-Advocate."

"On what basis?"

"On the indications of a ghost, a spook, as Lowee would say. That and the fact that Harry made the coffee."

Vledder nodded slowly to himself.

"They were faster than we."

"What do you mean by that?"

Vledder shrugged his shoulders.

"I told you at the time that we should have arrested Harry. I gave you, I think, some convincing arguments. He was the only one who could have benefited if the traces of poison immediately disappeared in soapy water."

DeKok gaped at his young friend.

"You really mean that?" he asked. "You really think that Harry Donkers killed Black Julie?"

Vledder nodded with emphasis.

"Yes, I do. From the very beginning, if you must know. I did understand, however, that you wanted to wait with his arrest until you had more evidence, but I never doubted his guilt. I'm convinced he's our perp."

DeKok continued to stare at Vledder.

"Convinced," he repeated. "Well, I promised the Commissaris that I would interrogate Donkers. I'm going to ask him if *you* can do the interrogation."

"Why?"

"Because," said DeKok, shaking his head, "I lack that conviction and therefore I'm not the right man for it." He stood up and ambled toward the door. "Ask Harry if he has an expensive girlfriend," he tossed over his shoulder.

"What expensive girlfriend?" Vledder called after him.

DeKok stood still and turned around.

"An expensive girlfriend can put strange ideas in a man's head."

* * *

DeKok walked down the Damrak, rain lashed his face and he pulled up the collar of his coat. It was bitter weather, too bitter for this time of the year. The dog days, he reflected, so called because at this time of the year, Sirius, the Dog Star, rises at the same time as the sun. The terraces were deserted and people huddled together at the streetcar stops. He turned off into Salt Alley and crossed the New Dike and eventually reached Duke Street. He looked at the cast-iron signs, screeching in the wind: *The Three Bottles*, *The Three Pills*, *The Three Candlesticks*. Here it was, in *Ye Three Roses*, that . . . how long ago? He peered inside. There was another girl behind the counter. Kristel was still in jail.*

He passed by and via Mole Alley reached Tower Gates. He felt sad and deserted. He tried to identify the source of his melancholy. Why had the Commissaris arrested Donkers without warning him? It had never happened before. Had he

---

* See: *DeKok and the Somber Nude*

been influenced by the JudgeAdvocate? How long had he been a cop? More than twenty-five years, most of it in Homicide. Why did he bother? He pulled a handkerchief from his pocket and wiped off his face.

It was strange, he thought, time and again people were able to confound him, confront him with almost insoluble problems. He put the handkerchief away. There was something strange about the murder of Black Julie, but what? There was no connection, no acceptable motive. It all seemed so senseless, as if she had been killed by accident. He stopped suddenly, thought about it. Was that possible? A strong gust blew his hat away. He watched it sail into the canal and shrugged his shoulders. He had at least a dozen more, all the same.

He crossed Lily Street toward Gentlemen's Canal. He halted in front of number eighty-eight and looked up. A fine example of an Amsterdam canal house with a well-preserved stair gable and the typical bluestone stoop. Slowly he climbed the few steps of the stoop until he reached the front door. A brass plate to one side announced: *Mathilda Lochem*. DeKok grinned and rang the doorbell.

It took several minutes before the door was carefully opened just a crack. In the narrow opening DeKok saw a cloud of gray hair and a set of penetrating, green eyes that observed him with suspicion. Slowly the door opened wider and DeKok saw a distinguished lady in an old-fashioned blue-gray, tweed suit. Her eyes were more friendly in the full light of day. They were softer, less suspicious. A smile of recognition lit up her face.

"What a surprise," she said gaily, "Inspector DeKok . . . in person."

DeKok smiled back at her.

She stepped back, inviting him in with a movement of her head. Then she closed the door behind him and carefully locked it and put a chain on the door. She gave him a worried look.

"You're all wet," she observed. "Take that wet coat off, quickly, before you catch a cold. It pays to be careful with this kind of weather. The dog days, you know . . . very treacherous."

DeKok nodded. His friendly face with the expression of a goodnatured boxer, became milder still.

"You remind me of my old Mother. My mother . . . she was a bit superstitious." He hung his coat from a peg. "She also, warned me about it. She didn't like this time of year. It must have been a premonition. She died during the dog days."

"Peacefully?"

DeKok stared into the distance. The memories of his Mother were dear to him.

"Very peaceful," he answered. "Bright and alert until the very last. She knew what was about to happen, but showed no fear. More like a resigned acceptance of the inevitable and a happy expectation of things to come."

Mathilda looked up at him.

"Everybody should have such a death."

DeKok nodded thoughtfully.

"It would certainly make my work a lot easier. I'm sure there would be less aggression, less violence, less *need* for murder."

Mathilda Lochem seemed to digest what he said.

"You mean," she said after a few seconds, "that a violent death does not offer the victim any time for reflection?"

DeKok nodded.

"What sort of chance did Black Julie have to prepare herself for death?"

Mathilda Lochem did not answer. She turned around and led the way down the corridor. Almost at the end, to the left, she opened a door to a cozy room decorated with some fine etchings and an old-fashioned railing for the display of plates. The furniture was predominantly *Jugendstil*, the German version of

Art Nouveau. The total effect was somehow perfect, without dissonants. She pointed invitingly at a small sofa and sat down across from him in the matching easy chair. She appeared calm, hands folded in her lap.

"You're interested in death?"

DeKok shook his head.

"Not in death," he denied, "but in life. Death is the end for most people. But for me, as a Police Inspector, it is the beginning . . . the beginning of a long search for the living killer."

She avoided his eyes.

"Is that the reason for your visit?"

DeKok smiled.

"My colleague, Vledder, described you as an intelligent and alert woman, who observed things. That seemed reason enough to get closer acquainted."

She blushed.

"You're still working on Black Julie's murder?"

"Indeed."

She looked shocked.

"But your own Commissaris and my brother arrested Harry Donkers, last night."

"Yes, they did," said DeKok evenly.

Mathilda Lochem swallowed, leaned closer toward her visitor.

"But you . . . you, eh, you don't think he's the murderer?"

DeKok shook his head.

"I can't find a motive. There simply isn't any. At least, not one I can recognize. What sort of relationship existed between Julie and Harry?"

She shrugged.

"As far as I know . . . none at all. Besides . . . nobody in the circle had any sort of relationship with Black Julie. Generally she was considered to be a bit . . . a bit common. Her reputation wasn't all that great, either. She was more or less tolerated because of her family relationship with Annette Leeuwenhoek. Only Jennifer, our medium, seemed to be charmed by her."

"Why?"

Mathilda Lochem made a sad gesture.

"I think it's because, on an astral level, they were on the same wavelength, so to speak." She paused, shook her head. There was a painful expression on her face when she continued. "As far as I can remember, Jennifer didn't want to . . . she . . . eh, she finally consented to the last session solely on my urging. If Harry Donkers, her nephew, has nothing to do with Julie's death, I don't think I can face her again."

DeKok cocked his head at her.

"Face her? A strange choice of words when applied to a woman who cannot see."

She gave him a strange look.

"But soon."

"Soon what?"

"Jennifer Jordan will soon be able to see again. Professor Hemming will operate next month. He's from out of town," she added with just a hint of contempt in her voice. To a real Amsterdammer, Holland consisted of two parts: Amsterdam and the provinces. Most Amsterdammers think about their city the way New Yorkers think about New York City.

"Oh?"

"Yes, according to the professor, Jennifer will be able to see again."

"That's happy news. How long has she been blind?"

Mathilda rubbed her forehead with the tips of her fingers, a meditative look on her face.

"That must have been at least fifteen years, by now. I remember it well. It was quite a shock when she suddenly became blind." She paused. "We are a bit scared of the operation," she whispered as an afterthought.

"Scared, why?"

She sighed.

"Over the years Jennifer has developed into an excellent medium, a medium who always quickly establishes contact with the other world, the spirit world. We . . . we in the circle, think that her blindness has something to do with her sensitivity."

DeKok nodded his understanding.

"And now you wonder if she'll be as eh, . . . as sensitive *after* the operation?"

"Exactly, we do not want to lose our medium."

DeKok gave her a sharp look.

"Not even if that means she'll be able to see again, after having been deprived of sight for so long?"

She avoided his eyes again.

"You're right . . . it's a selfish thought."

DeKok stood up.

"You will tell your brother, the Judge-Advocate, about this conversation?"

She shook her head.

"I will not try to influence him again. I know he listens to me. He has done so since he was a child." She followed him into the corridor. "I hope, for you and for me, that you're wrong about Harry Donkers."

DeKok did not respond. He pulled on his wet raincoat and automatically grabbed for his hat. Then he remembered it was somewhere in the Lily Canal. He raked a hand through his hair. Before he opened the door he gave her a last look.

"Mrs. Lochem . . . how do you take your coffee?"

"Black . . . just black."

10

DeKok walked back toward Warmoes Street. He liked to walk and by preference walked wherever he could, even on duty. If Vledder was not around to drive him, he had been known, on rare occasions, to use a bicycle. But even this ubiquitous transportation of the Dutch, was really too modern and above all, too mechanical for DeKok. He always maintained that he could get around the inner city of Amsterdam faster on foot than by any other means. And he often proved it, because DeKok knew alleys, short-cuts and little known bridges that appeared on few maps. Also, he maintained, a nice walk gave him plenty of time to think and there was little enough of that, these days.

It had stopped raining and a watery sun came peeking from behind silver lined clouds. The world around him seemed more cheerful, less depressed, and it lifted his heart. Deep down he nurtured a feeling that despite his somber thoughts, he would soon be able to unravel the mysteries surrounding the murder in seance. He worried about the motive. As if on cue, the sun disappeared behind the clouds. He shook his head as he walked on. No matter what theory he tried, he kept getting stuck on the why of it all. Why was Black Julie killed?

As he entered the station, Meindert Post raised his voice. DeKok came closer.

"You know, Meindert," he said amicably, "I wonder how much longer the walls of this station will be able to hold up against your constant roar. One of these days the whole building will come down around our ears."

Meindert Post laughed and pointed toward the ceiling.

"Guy waiting for you."

"So, Vledder is in, isn't he?"

"Sure, but the guy insisted on seeing you."

"What sort of guy?"

Meindert shrugged his shoulders.

"Big guy, he limps."

DeKok smiled and climbed the stairs, two treads at a time. Outside the detective room he found Gerard Klaver. As soon as the ex-construction worker saw DeKok, he came to his feet. His rough-hewn face was expressionless.

"I came to talk to you," he said gravely.

DeKok shook hands with the big man.

"How do you do?" he asked, genuine interest in his voice.

Gerard ignored the question.

"Do you know yet, who killed my Jane?"

DeKok's face fell.

"Not yet. And I must admit that I don't see any hope at this time."

Klaver nodded slowly to himself.

"Jane'll be buried tomorrow. There are a few of her sisters and some family of mine." He looked up, a stubborn look on his face. "I warn you, DeKok, if Charles Leeuwenhoek, or his sister, show their face at the cemetery, I'll personally put a knife through them." He groped in a pocket and showed a slim stiletto. He pressed his lips together as he looked at DeKok. "I've bought this especially for that. Just in case they show up. You can take it away from me, that's your right. But I'll just get another as soon as I leave here."

DeKok shrugged his shoulders.

"That's silly. I can hardly prohibit a man from attending his wife's funeral."

Gerard Klaver waved his arms in the air, the knife barely missed DeKok. His face was red and his lips quivered.

"She isn't his wife," he exclaimed. "She never was."

DeKok placed a calming hand on the big man's shoulders.

"Come on," he said soothingly. "Come with me. Let's talk."

He led Klaver with gentle persuasion to one of the small interrogation rooms and held a chair for the invalid. Then DeKok sat down across from the man, who still had the knife in one hand.

"I don't think," said DeKok calmly, "that your hate for Charles Leeuwenhoek is justified. I would think about that, if I were you. I had a long conversation with Charles and I'm certain that he's *not* responsible for the death of Jane in any way, shape, or form."

Klaver spread his arms in a gesture of despair.

"Who is?"

DeKok did not answer at once, but studied his visitor. Slowly, reluctantly, Klaver placed the knife on the table. DeKok nodded silent approval.

"There must be," said DeKok, "certain hints in Jane's life that can lead us to the killer." He looked intently at the construction worker. "You've known her since she was seventeen."

Klaver nodded. The angry look on his face disappeared, replaced by something more dreamy.

"I knew everything about her."

DeKok leaned closer, creating an atmosphere of confidentiality.

"Everything . . . and there was nothing that could connect to her death?"

"Yes, the attempts on her life by the Leeuwenhoek family. I told you about that."

DeKok nodded.

"But other than that? I mean . . . did Jane ever tell you things from the time *before* you knew her?"

Gerard Klaver looked sad.

"It wasn't all that interesting. Poverty was king." He paused. "Whenever we were a bit short, Jane used to say: 'If the old Lord was still alive, I'd pay him a visit,' but of course, he wasn't."

"The old Lord?" prompted DeKok.

Klaver sighed deeply.

"Madness . . . nothing but madness. You know how women are, sometimes . . . romantic with wild dreams of fame and fortune."

"What was the matter with that Lord?"

Klaver moved uneasily in his chair, pushed the knife to one side of the table.

"Ach," he said reluctantly, "a kitchen maid story . . . no more. One of those romances you read about in . . . by, what's her name, the English lady. You see, Jane's mother was a whore all her life. She started young. According to Jane, her mother was only fourteen when she brought johns home. Together with her cousin, Clara. They just took the johns home and the parents, Jane's grandparents, looked the other way."

"They profited from it."

Gerard Klaver nodded agreement.

"Exactly. Those were hard times. You could hardly blame the parents. It was bail or drown. There was hardly any work and everybody had too many mouths to feed. From what I hear, Jane's mother and her cousin were good-looking girls. I can believe that, you could see it by looking at Jane. Jane looked like her mother. And those two could sing a little, Jane's mother and Clara, I mean . . . not good enough to be professionals, but good enough to sing in bars and honky-tonks. That's when they must have met that Lord, an Englishman with an itch and a lot of dough."

"How did that end?"

Klaver leaned his elbows on the table.

"I don't know, exactly. I wasn't all that interested, as I said. They were just stories, tales from the past. Anyway, it seems that Clara married the guy eventually. Whatever . . . after Clara married, Jane's mother would send Jane to get some money from the Lord, from time to time."

"And that worked?"

Klaver smiled.

"I think so. That's why she used to say: 'If the old Lord was still alive, I'd pay him a visit.' At least, I think so."

DeKok rubbed his face with a flat hand. The old history intrigued him. He thought he saw a glimmer of a connection. For the first time since the investigation had started.

"That old Lord is dead . . . is Clara still alive?"

Klaver shook his head.

"I don't think she's still alive. Jane's mother died years ago and according to Jane, her mother and Clara were about the same age."

"Do you know Jennifer Jordan?"

Gerard Klaver made a vague gesture.

"I've heard the name."

DeKok gave him a sharp look.

"She's blind and she was the medium at the seance where Jane died."

Klaver gave a short, barking laugh.

"Jane never told me anything about that spirit stuff. She knew I didn't believe in it and that I was against it. I didn't like to see her go, so we never really talked about it."

"Did you ever attend a seance?"

"No, Jane tried a few times to get me to go along, but I always refused. I'm not the sort of man who likes to be fooled."

DeKok stood up and looked down at the big, square man with the remarkable red hair.

"How did Jane drink her coffee?"

Klaver was surprised. He looked up with a question in his eyes.

"How did she drink her coffee?" he repeated.

"Yes," said DeKok.

"Lots of milk and sugar."

DeKok nodded slowly, as if he had known it all along. Then he helped Klaver to his feet and led him to the stairs.

"Can you manage the stairs?" he asked, concern in his voice.

"Oh, yes, I'm slow, but steady."

DeKok respected his pride and shook hands warmly.

"Thanks," said DeKok.

"For what?"

"For the knife . . . you left it on the table."

Klaver slapped his pocket and then grinned, a bit abashed.

"Yes."

"I don't think you'll be buying another one," said DeKok with a smile.

Klaver shook his head and turned toward the stairs.

* * *

Vledder showed his surprise.

"Klaver told you that?"

DeKok nodded.

"It came out when I asked him if Jane had ever told him anything about the time *before* he met her."

"Just like that?"

"More or less, at least I think so. Klaver isn't the kind of man to dissemble."

"Well, that fits with what Lowee told us . . . that Jennifer is supposed to be the child of an English Lord."

"Exactly."

"That could mean that Jennifer and Black Julie have known each other since they were children. At least . . . we can *assume* that. After all, their mothers were cousins."

"And partners in prostitution. But it explains why Jennifer, in the words of Mathilda, was so charmed by Julie."

Vledder looked thoughtful.

"In that case her sudden death must have affected Jennifer more than she showed."

DeKok nodded approvingly.

"Very good, there should have been more of a reaction than was apparent."

Vledder rubbed his hair.

"She was cool, almost reserved," he recalled. "And, in light of what we now know, that was strange. Especially if you take into consideration that she, just like Annette Leeuwenhoek, must have realized immediately who was meant with the message 'Jane dies.' I wonder who else knew." He paused and absent-mindedly stroked the keys of his keyboard, as if trying to seek help from the computer. "The more I think about it," continued Vledder, "the more I feel that the motive is somehow connected to the trio of Annette Leeuwenhoek, Jennifer Jordan and Harry Donkers."

"How?"

Vledder shrugged his shoulders, an irritated look on his face.

"I can't figure that out, yet. But I think it might be important to take a close look at the background of all three."

"Did you interrogate Harry Donkers?"

"Yes," nodded Vledder, "for more than two hours."

"And?"

The young Inspector shook his head.

"He denies everything . . . vigorously and consistently. I tried everything, but he's sticking to the story he gave us in the beginning."

DeKok smiled maliciously.

"Perhaps the spirits made a mistake and Harry is innocent, after all."

Vledder reacted in an unusually fierce way.

"The spirits were right when they pointed Jane out as the victim."

DeKok looked up with amazement.

"You really believe that the spirits of the departed hang around to send us messages?"

Vledder ignored the question.

"After my interrogation of Donkers," he said, "I reported to the Commissaris. He consulted with the Judge-Advocate. Despite Harry's complete denial, they don't want to release him. The Judge-Advocate has issued an official arrest warrant."

"On suspicion of murder?"

Vledder nodded.

"Yes, on the same grounds as his original arrest, which was, as you well know, only good for forty-eight hours. The Judge-Advocate will file definitive charges as soon as possible."

A woman appeared in the door opening of the detective room. She turned toward the nearest desk with an occupant and asked a question. The detective at that desk pointed toward

DeKok's desk. The woman was dressed in a dark-blue suit of a simple cut. It looked a bit like a Salvation Army uniform, without the usual distinguishing embellishments. The black, graying hair had been combed straight back and ended in a bun.

DeKok recognized her at once and hastened to meet her half way.

"Mrs. Vanwal," he greeted her heartily. "What can we do for you?"

She gave him a tired smile.

"A lot, I hope. First of all, I should tell you that I'm not here of my own volition. Jennifer asked me to look you up. In a way, I'm here in her name."

DeKok led her to his desk and held the chair for her.

"But you could have saved yourself the trip," he said easily. "Mrs. Jordan could have called us. We would have come at once."

Christine Vanwal raised a hand in surrender.

"Jennifer . . . I mean . . . we have little experience with the forces of law and order."

DeKok grinned infectiously. It was the grin for which he was famous. It made him look happy and boyish and people who experienced the full force of that grin tended to forget he was a cop. He became everybody's favorite uncle. Vledder noticed with interest that Christine Vanwal seemed to fall under the spell as easily as so many others before her.

"No force," said DeKok, "and precious little order. Please don't distress yourself."

She smiled, a bit more brightly.

"Well," she said, "you know."

"Of course I do," said DeKok hastily. His face became serious. "Please tell me what bothers Mrs. Jordan?"

Christine Vanwal looked at Vledder and then at DeKok.

"It's about Harry," she said shyly. "Jennifer is convinced he's innocent. And I agree with her. Therefore, Mr. DeKok, we urgently request you to set him free."

DeKok spread his hands helplessly.

"I did not arrest him. The Commissaris, my chief, and the Judge-Advocate have arrested him. Besides, Jennifer helped with the unmasking, if I may call it that. According to my information, the spirits themselves, pointed to Harry Donkers as the guilty party."

Christine shook her head.

"It's all the fault of Mathilda Lochem. She insisted that we have a seance with your Commissaris and her brother, the Judge-Advocate, present. Jennifer refused, at first. She's never at ease when there are strangers in the circle. It becomes more difficult for her to reach the other world."

"But she agreed?"

Christine Vanwal lowered her head.

"It was almost blackmail."

"By whom?"

"Mathilda."

DeKok was confused.

"How?"

"When Jennifer refused, Mathilda asked if she was perhaps interested in shielding the killer." She swallowed. "Then Jennifer agreed."

DeKok stared over her shoulder.

"That was not nice," he said at last.

Christine shook her head.

"No, not nice at all. Nasty, I thought. Jennifer was very upset, completely confused. That's why it went wrong."

"What?"

"The seance that evening." She made a wild gesture. "Jennifer knew very well that Mathilda's hint was aimed at her nephew, Harry. She spoke about a murderer, referring to a man . . . and Harry was the only man among us. Jennifer was so preoccupied with that, that the name 'Harry' just automatically seemed to appear on the board."

"Because of the spirits?"

"No," denied Christine indignantly. "*not* because of the spirits. That's a misconception. Jennifer was not in contact with the spirit world at that time. She was in contact with her own spirit. Her own spirit dominated at that time, you understand? Her thoughts were so occupied with her nephew, that the Board automatically indicated his name." She stopped and coughed. "Then, after the board, when the Commissaris and the Judge-Advocate concentrated their attention on Harry, Jennifer had neither the courage, nor the strength, to explain what had happened."

"So she allowed him to be arrested?"

Christine nodded slowly to herself.

"Jennifer simply did not react at all. It was several hours before she realized what had happened. She thought they would soon discover, the police, that is, that they had made a mistake. But when Harry didn't come back, she realized it was serious. That's when she called Mathilda, to try and get Harry set free, with the help of her brother."

"And?"

"Mathilda called back to say that her brother was adamant and would not allow Harry to go free. He said that the case is still being investigated."

DeKok showed resignation.

"I can't tell you much more than that. I simply lack the authority to set Harry free. And the way things are at the moment, I doubt that the Judge-Advocate will change his mind. Unless . . ." He stopped talking abruptly, his sharp gaze searched her face. "Unless," he continued, "the murder*ess* is unmasked in time."

"Murder*ess*?"

DeKok grimaced.

"If it isn't Harry . . . the killer is a woman."

Christine Vanwal looked at him without guile.

"You're right," she said decisively. "It *has* to be a woman. I discussed it at length with Jennifer and I told her that if we want to help Harry, we have to discover who killed Black Julie. Jennifer agreed. That's why we'll have another seance tonight. Closed . . . just the regular members. All the women have promised to attend. Jennifer is now preparing herself and if the spirits are willing and the seance has results, you'll be the first to know."

She stood up. Calm, self-possessed. She considered the interview terminated.

DeKok walked her to the door, then he shook hands.

"What time is the seance?"

"Eight o'clock."

"And when will it be finished?"

She bit her lip.

"Ten, maybe . . . half past ten, or so."

DeKok nodded agreeably.

"My colleague and I will stay in the office until eleven. So you can reach us here. Please give Mrs. Jordan my best regards and wish her strength."

Christine sighed.

"She'll need it," she said with concern. "This business, this whole affair . . . is no good for her." She walked toward the stairs.

DeKok called after her.

"Mrs. Vanwal, just one more question . . . how do you take your coffee?"

She was taken aback.

"Little sugar . . . a drop of milk."

"And Jennifer?"

She hesitated, seemed suddenly unsure of herself.

"Jennifer? Extra sugar and cream."

* * *

Vledder looked skeptical.

"And you will wait?" he asked, disbelief in his voice. "You'll wait for the result of the seance? I thought you had no faith in those spiritualistic shenanigans?"

DeKok shook his head.

"I don't. The seance is unimportant. I am interested in the gathering of those nine women, of whom *one* has a murder on her conscience. I'm sure that during the last seance, when the Commissaris and Maitre Lochem were present, they would have been guarded in their remarks. I hope that the dam now bursts. That something will be revealed."

"What?"

"I don't know," answered DeKok, annoyance in his tone of voice. "But something has to happen, something will be said. It's very frustrating that we still don't know *why* she was killed."

He stood up and started pacing the floor to help him gather his thoughts. Suddenly he stopped.

"Does Harry have an expensive girlfriend?"

Vledder smiled a bitter smile.

"I don't know if she's expensive, but he has a girlfriend. For some time. I allowed him to call her, this morning. He asked for it and I didn't see the harm. Her name is Viola Weinbaum and she has a condo in Purmerend. Harry Donkers bought it for her two years ago . . . paid in cash."

DeKok was flabbergasted.

"That must have cost him at least a hundred, maybe a hundred and fifty thousand."

Vledder nodded.

"And our friend drives a brand-new Jaguar. The doorman of the condo building told me that. I talked to him by phone. Apparently Harry visits his girlfriend three, or four times per week. Sometimes he stays the night but not always."

"Does he have a job, a regular income?"

"Not as far as I know. Apart from his little trips to Viola, he seems to reside in the canal house with his aunt. Perhaps we can assume that Jennifer takes care of his monetary needs from time to time."

They both fell silent. DeKok walked over and sat down on Vledder's desk, a morose look on his face.

"What about the report from forensics?" asked DeKok suddenly.

"Came in this morning."

"Well?"

Vledder opened a drawer of his desk and produced a folder. He placed the folder in front of him, while he did something incomprehensible to his computer terminal. He glanced at the screen and then opened the folder.

"You were right. In addition to traces of cyanide, there was also a considerable amount of morphine in Jane's body." He glanced at his screen as if to verify the information in the report. "The toxicological research was aimed at morphine because most *psycholeptica stimulantia* and *hypnotica* in the body is quickly transf . . ." He stopped when DeKok held up his hand.

"Spare me the jargon," said DeKok gruffly. "I'm not interested in the methodology, whether they first looked at the liver and then something else, or whatever. What's the bottom line?"

"Average concentrations in fluids and body parts were about five and ten micrograms, respectively per cc."

DeKok glanced at the report.

"And they needed five pages to tell you that."

Vledder replaced the folder in his desk drawer.

"It's quite a lot," he remarked. "I checked it against the usual concentrations found in people who died of a drug overdose and it's virtually the same. Small wonder that Black Julie keeled over almost instantly."

"Unfortunately it's no longer all that hard to get your hands on large quantities of hard drugs," remarked DeKok cynically. "Although the number of addicts has diminished rapidly, the supplies are still readily available. The only difference is that now they practically give it away."

The phone on DeKok's desk rang. Vledder leaned over and lifted the receiver. DeKok watched him and saw his young friend pale.

"What is it?"

Without another word, Vledder replaced the receiver and stared in the distance.

DeKok shook him gently.

"What is it?" he repeated.

Vledder swallowed.

"Jennifer Jordan . . . she's dead."

11

A decrepit Police VW Beetle stopped on the side of the canal and cautiously parked between the old, crooked elms. Detective-Inspector DeKok hoisted himself out of the cramped confines of the vehicle with some difficulty and stepped on the narrow strip of pavement that had remained clear between the car and the edge of the canal. Leaning on the roof of the car he looked up at the house. The graceful neck gable blended splendidly with the two stair gables of the houses next door.

Vledder locked the car and leaned his back against it. For a moment they remained thus, in silence, staring at the house. Then they crossed the quay toward the narrow sidewalk and Vledder preceded DeKok up the few steps toward the front door.

Just like last time, the heavy front door was ajar. They pushed it open. Through the pink marble corridor they reached the stairs. Vledder climbed the stairs quickly, DeKok followed at a more sedate pace.

This time Harry Donkers was not waiting for them, but Agatha Cologne stood at the top of the stairs. Her eyes flashed angrily at the two Inspectors as she pressed her lips together into a thin line of disapproval.

DeKok lifted his hat.

"How many more murders do there have to be?" Her creaky voice dripped venom. "If you don't arrest her now, I'll file charges for dereliction of duty."

DeKok feigned surprise.

"Who?"

Agatha Cologne snorted contemptuously. The gesture seemed to come naturally to her.

"Annette Leeuwenhoek, who else? Now she's killed poor Jennifer."

DeKok ignored her remarks and passed by her. At the end of the corridor he opened the door to the low, intimate room. He had a momentary sense of *deja vu* as he saw the women, grouped together near the windows. The whispering stopped when the two cops entered the room.

DeKok's gaze roamed around the room as he stepped inside. To the left, next to a painting by Monet, he stopped. The tips of his fingers caressed the canvass. Then he walked on.

The big, round, oaken table stood in the center of the room, nine chairs around it. The chairs were empty. Right in front of him, across the table, one of the chairs was pulled aside. Next to the chair, on the Berber carpet, was the body of a woman. She was supine, the legs slightly spread and the blind eyes were wide open. DeKok looked down on her. The sight of the dead woman in the black toga touched him strangely. *You don't steal from no blind person, you just don't.* Lowee's words came in his mind. But who would give a deadly poison to a defenseless, blind woman? He looked at the women near the window. There she was. But who?

He motioned to Vledder.

"Smell her mouth."

Vledder kneeled down next to the dead woman. For just a moment. Then he rose, his face even.

"Bitter almonds," he said hoarsely.

DeKok looked at the table top. It was empty, cleared away. Suddenly he turned around and rushed to the kitchen. The women seemed surprised, but Vledder had a sudden look of realization on his face. DeKok reached the kitchen and stared at the sink. Eight cups and saucers were immersed in soapy water.

Slowly he walked back to the room. The women were still next to the windows, as if on parade. He stopped a few feet away from them and planted his feet wide apart, He crossed his arms across his chest and with the face of a thundercloud he barked at them.

"Who did the dishes?"

Agatha Cologne stepped forward, DeKok towered over her small figure.

"I did."

"Why?"

She shrugged her shoulders as if the answer was obvious.

"Harry wasn't here," she said, "and *somebody* had to clear away the mess. I could hardly leave the dirty cups standing around."

DeKok sighed, deflated. The typical syndrome of the Dutch housewife, he thought. Painfully clean and neat. What could one expect in a country where the housewives regularly scrub the sidewalks in front of their houses with hot water and soap. DeKok had several colleagues who were married to women like that. They'd wash the dishes after every use. If you had three cups of coffee in their house, you got a clean cup three times. Thankfully his own wife was less fanatic. In his own house magazines were allowed to pile up in disorder and more often than not the newspaper was still on the floor the next day where he had put it after reading. Still, he reflected, even his own house was a place where, as the Dutch said, *you could eat off the floor.*

It was not the first time that an investigation had been slowed down by the Dutch passion for neatness. It was not limited to women. He had known cops who had to be restrained from straightening out a corpse, because it looked so "messy" otherwise.

He motioned for Agatha to step back. His sharp gaze examined the women with the intrusive, brutal frankness of a cop, impervious to other people's feelings. Their faces were expressionless, although some of them fidgeted uneasily. Only Mathilda Lochem had a faintly amused smile on her face. DeKok thought about his old Mother. *My boy,* she used to say, *you can look people in the face, but you can't look in their heart.* His early youth had been peppered with sayings like that. But she was right. In retrospect, she had always been right. It was a shame that it had taken him so many years to be convinced of that. With an effort he suppressed the thoughts of his mother and dug his feet solidly into the carpet.

"One of you," he said accusingly, "possibly in concert with others . . . now has two murders on her conscience. As long as I don't know who is responsible for these reprehensible killings, I have no choice but to suspect you all. Frankly, I'm tempted to arrest the lot of you, lock you up in one of the medieval cells at Warmoes Street station until the real killer, and/or her accomplices, reveal themselves."

Mathilda Lochem snorted.

"You don't have the right."

DeKok looked at her, fire in his eyes.

"If your brother, the esteemed Judge-Advocate," he lambasted her, "takes it upon himself to arrest Harry Donkers on far more nebulous charges, then I *will* have the right to lock up a bunch of women who are clearly implicated in *both* murders."

Annette Leeuwenhoek stepped forth.

"That's absurd," she protested, "and you know it. We're not in cahoots. We're just members of a spiritualistic circle from among whom two women have been poisoned. You cannot arrest all eight of us . . . hold all of us responsible for the acts of just one of us."

DeKok stretched out a hand toward her.

"How do you know there's only one?"

Annette Leeuwenhoek shook her head.

"I don't know," she said calmly. "But *you* were speaking of a conspiracy. A conspiracy means forethought, malice aforethought, I believe is the proper expression. Well, I for one, have never participated in such a conspiracy."

A vehement murmur followed these words. Cries of approval and agreement. Marie Vaart, a small, blonde woman stepped forward.

"It was just a speech confessing how powerless you are." Her voice was deliberate. "You're faced with the task of solving two murders and apparently you don't have enough evidence to find the perpetrator. I'm sorry about that. But it is less than elegant to try and solve the case with threats."

DeKok was angry. Vledder came closer, ready to intervene. DeKok, like many of the usually so placid Dutch, was prone to sudden flashes of rage and passion that resembled the actions of a Beserker. It did not happen often, but Vledder had seen DeKok in such a mood before and took no chances. DeKok pressed his lips together and snorted heavily. With an effort he controlled himself and Vledder relaxed slightly.

"Less than elegant?" roared DeKok, finally venting his anger in sheer volume. "Less than elegant?" He swallowed. "How elegant do you consider the poisoning of a defenseless, blind woman?" With a look of disgust he turned away from the women and looked at Vledder.

"Will you finish up here?"

Vledder nodded.

"I already heard the ambulance, outside. I'll just wait for the Coroner."

DeKok threw another angry glance over his shoulder. The women were deep in conversation next to the windows. He turned back toward Vledder.

"I'll see you at the station, later." He waved at the gathering crowd of policemen and added: "You deal with them."

"Where are you going?"

There was determined look on DeKok's face when he answered.

"Looking for evidence."

* * *

When DeKok stepped outside, he looked back at the house. Behind three narrow windows he saw a light and the silhouettes of the women. He recognized a few of them. Behind those windows, he knew, festered a dark conspiracy that had already taken two lives. Black Julie . . . too full of life to die so young and Jennifer Jordan. He was surprised to realize that he had half expected the death of the medium. It was as if he had a premonition that was not recognized until now. But it was more or less to be expected, he scolded himself. He wondered if he could have done anything to prevent it. As always, he blamed himself. Then he wondered if there would be more victims and if so, who would be next? He nodded at the constable guarding the door and turned around.

Thoughtfully he walked along the narrow sidewalk. Apart from the various police vehicles that had brought the personnel from the Technical Service, it was quiet on the canal, a bit uncanny. The noise of distant traffic seemed subdued. A cat dozed on one of the stoops, one eye on DeKok. He hardly noticed the animal. He was concentrating on the case. Again he wondered if he could have prevented Jennifer's death. He felt he should have been able to do so, but could not think of a way.

Should he have prohibited further seances in order to save a potential victim? He could not have done that. Apart from the constitutional right to freedom of religion, he would not have been able to enforce it. There were simply no Laws or regulations that would have allowed him to act. Impossible. The only solution was to unmask the murderess as soon as possible. But what could be considered as soon as possible?

From Emperors Canal he crossed the bridge toward Princes Street and from there along a short length of Princes Canal toward North Market. Behind the Reformed Church, he stopped in front of a small house with a big, high window. In the middle of the window where the words *Peter Karstens* in elegant scroll lettering. Underneath, in smaller letters, he read: *Painter- Artist.*

DeKok looked at his watch and noted the time. Well past eleven. He rubbed the bridge of his nose with a little finger. "An unchristian hour for a visit," he said to himself. But that did not prevent him from giving a yank on the brass bell pull. Inside the house he heard the rattle of the bell, loud and insistent. DeKok was not worried about the noise. He had known the occupant for a long time and knew his nocturnal habits.

It took about two minutes and then the door was opened by a man with dark-blond hair, dressed in sweat pants and a black, gleaming silk shirt. He frowned until he recognized DeKok.

"DeKok," exclaimed the man with a mixture of surprise and delight. "My goodness, what's up? What an ungodly hour to arrest someone."

DeKok laughed.

"I'm not here to arrest you, Peter," he said pleasantly. "Not this time. I came for a visit."

The artist hesitated for a moment. Then he performed a slight bow and spread wide his arms. It was a gracious, old-fashioned gesture and DeKok approved thoroughly.

"Trusty henchman of Capitalism," joked Peter, "enter my humble abode."

DeKok gave him a withering look.

"Please be careful how you express yourself. I'm not a henchman of Capitalism. I'm a henchman of the Law."

The artist pulled on his short VanDyke beard.

"Isn't that just about the same thing?"

DeKok shook his head and smiled. He entered and looked around the high, spacious room. It was almost dark. The only light cane from a streetlight across the street. It threw long shadows among easels and half-finished paintings. The walls, too, were covered with paintings.

Karstens led the way to a staircase at the end of the space that led downward. After a short corridor at the bottom of the stairs, they stepped into a comfortable, cozy room with a low ceiling. A rough wooden table supported a set of candles, a few bottles of wine and two crystal glasses. An easel with a cloth draped over the painting stood in one corner.

DeKok looked around and discovered a young woman in the shadows. She rested elegantly on a wide, leather settee surrounded by extinguished spotlights. He had not noticed her before, but now he took a closer look. She was extremely beautiful, he thought. In the half-light of the candles she had an uncommon, ethereal beauty. Her ivory colored skin glowed in the soft light. A shawl, or long scarf, was draped across her lap and covered most of the settee. A discreet nail polish decorated her toenails. Long, wavy black hair descended in luxurious ripples down to her naked chest. Two perfect breasts, topped by big, hard, red nipples poked proudly through the veil of hair. As she moved DeKok noticed that the shawl was her only clothing. It made him dizzy. His puritanical soul was always a bit confused when confronted with such blatant sexuality.

Peter Karstens waved casually in her direction.

"Allow me to introduce you . . . Maria . . . after painting, the love of my life."

Slowly she came to her feet, tossed the hair to the back of her head with an impatient gesture and unashamedly displayed herself as the long scarf trailed from one hand behind her. She stepped forward with the agility of a cat and shook hands with DeKok. Her breasts bobbed pleasingly. DeKok looked in her eyes.

"DeKok," announced Karstens in a declarative voice, "Inspector of Police and a jewel in the crown of Amsterdam's forces of law and order."

DeKok ignored the announcement and the tone. He looked deep into Maria's eyes and noted a hint of amusement in the dark orbs. With a slight pressure, she released his hand and went back to the settee. She crossed slender legs and pulled the wrap around her shoulders, covering her front at the same time. Suddenly, with the wrap around her, she looked as chaste as a nun, but still as beautiful.

DeKok shook his head, as if to clear his vision. Then he looked at his host. Karstens was an artist who lived in a kind of uneasy truce with the rest of society. He was a buccaneer with the untamed soul of the true artist. He did not fit in an ordered society. Perhaps that was why the man was dear to DeKok's heart. Both men, at times, were convinced they had been born several hundred years too late.

Karstens pointed at the table.

"A wonderful Burgundy," he said. "A *Hospice de Nuits St. Georges* from an especially good year, blessed by God. Ripened, picked, pressed and aged for the delight of real men . . ." He paused and placed a hand on Maria's knee. ". . . and women." There was jubilation in his voice as he continued. "Women and wine . . . impossible to think of a more inspired combination."

"Ham and eggs?" suggested Maria drily. Her voice was as beautiful as her body.

Karstens ignored the remark and lifted a bottle.

"You will have a glass, won't you?"

"Most assuredly," confirmed DeKok.

Peter Karstens poured carefully, but generously. The light from the candle gave the wine an extra deep, rich color.

DeKok accepted the glass and tasted. The wine was indeed superb. While the liquid poured like velvet down his throat, DeKok gave Karstens a good look. He guessed that the artist had emptied more than a few glasses already. Peter seemed in a happy, excited mood. He sat down next to Maria and handed her a glass as well. She sipped delicately.

"Why are you here?" asked Karstens.

DeKok did not answer at once, but nodded discreetly in Maria's direction.

"Does she ... eh, excuse me, my dear, but ... does she know?"

Peter Karstens laughed uproariously.

"It's because of her that I've come as far as I have. She's always telling me *Peter, if you had lived in the 17th Century, your paintings would be worth millions.*" He scratched behind his ear. "Well, I'm living now, I thought, why shouldn't I make millions off paintings from the 17th Century?"

DeKok smiled.

"You still do that?"

Peter took a thoughtful sip from his wine.

"I presume," he said carefully, "that you are here as a friend, not as a cop."

DeKok looked serious.

"I'm here as a friend ... *and* a cop."

Peter shook his head.

"Impossible. Those are irreconcilable differences." He paused and gave DeKok a long, hard look. "If you're here as a friend, empty your glass and I'll pour again. But if you're here as a cop, as a representative of the Law . . . tell me what's on your mind."

DeKok slowly finished his glass and then placed it on the rough, wooden table. He looked resignedly at the artist.

"It's up to you if you want to pour again."

Karstens hesitated for just a few seconds. Then, in response to a hardly noticeable nudge from Maria, he stood up, a wide grin on his face. He poured with style and handed the full glass to DeKok.

"You know, DeKok," he said pensively, looking at Maria who gave him an approving smile, "as a cursed representative of the Law, you're not all that bad."

DeKok grinned in appreciation. The full-bodied wine warmed his innards and he would have been happy to forget all about the reason for his visit. Preferably he would have liked to pull up a chair, put his feet up and chat away the rest of the night. But the memory of dead Jennifer Jordan brought him back to reality. With a sigh he replaced his glass and leaned closer.

"I told you once," he began, "that I have a great admiration for the Impressionists . . . Monet, Renoir, Cezanne . . . Toulouse-Lautrec. I very much appreciate the work of those artists. So full of color. For a simple civil servant, like me, they are, of course, completely out of reach. Otherwise I wouldn't mind covering my walls with them." He looked sad. "I satisfy myself with a number of good reproductions."

Peter laughed happily.

"No problem. You want me to paint you some Renoirs? Monets, perhaps? Just tell me what you want."

DeKok pulled his lower lip and let it plop back. He saw the look on Maria's face and quickly interrupted the annoying gesture.

"You think you could?" he asked, doubt in his voice. "I mean . . . just like real, so that you can't tell the difference between yours and a real Monet, or Renoir?"

Karstens looked insulted.

"What those boys did at the end of the last Century," he said morosely, "is nothing. Half of what they knew I've already forgotten." He paused. "Although . . . I have to admit that they did some wonderful work."

DeKok nodded agreement.

"What could have happened to all of it? I mean, in total it must have been a considerable body of work. There must have been hundreds . . . thousands, maybe."

The artist shrugged his shoulders.

"In the beginning they couldn't even *give* their work away. They were ignored. The *public* shrugged them off. They went for a song. Sometimes they paid their rent with paintings . . . they used to charge by the *size* of the canvass, can you believe that? Later, as they became better known, especially the British Galleries bought a lot."

DeKok bit his lower lip.

"And in Holland?"

Karstens shook his head.

"Not too many wound up here, I'm afraid. But don't despair. Maybe you'll get lucky. As I said, at first few people realized the value of those paintings. I'm convinced that there are a good many still hidden away, gathering dust in some forgotten corner of an attic, or whatever."

DeKok laughed.

"Have *you* ever done a Monet?"

"Sure."

"On commission?"

"That, too."

"When?"

The artist rubbed his forehead, trying to concentrate.

"A few years ago, I think. A copy job. The order was for two Renoirs and a Monet."

DeKok held his breath.

"Who gave you the commission?"

Again the artist took time to think.

"A woman, I think . . . an older lady with long, gray hair."

DeKok swallowed.

"You remember the name?"

Peter turned toward Maria.

"What did you do with the cards?" he asked.

Maria stood up and circled the couch. DeKok followed her with his eyes and the sight took his breath away. Although the wrap covered her adequately in the front, in the back her hourglass figure was bare from just below her shoulder blades to her heels. With slightly swaying hips she went to a sideboard and rummaged in a tray. She picked up a number of business cards and visiting cards and turned back to face the room. The result was startling. Viewed from the back she had been almost totally nude, but now she was covered from neck to feet by the long wrap that had been draped over her shoulders. She ignored the effect she had on both men and handed the stack of cards to Peter. With a graceful movement she resumed her former position.

Karstens shuffled the card until he found what he wanted

"It's got to be here," he murmured. "I'm sure of it. I saved it." Finally he looked up with a gleam of triumph in his eyes. "What did I tell you? Here it is! Annette Leeuwenhoek."

12

DeKok gazed at Vledder with concern. The young man looked defeated and discouraged. There were red rims around his eyes and his blond hair was disheveled. His collar was loose and the necktie was askew. DeKok had never seen him in such a state of disarray. Vledder was always neatly dressed and well groomed. The old man took a chair across from his young colleague.

"Well," he began cautiously, "learn anything new tonight?"

Vledder shook his head sadly.

"Nothing, not an inch closer to an answer. Those women were even more closed mouthed than before. Nobody had noticed anything beforehand, nobody had any suspicions as to who could have done it, and nobody knew about any motive. Except for Agatha Cologne . . . she insisted I arrest Annette Leeuwenhoek, then and there. There was quite an exchange of words about that. Apart from that, everybody was very shocked, upset and indignant."

"Indignant?"

"With you. After you left, you should have heard them . . . tongues really wagged there for a while. The very idea that you dared threaten them all with incarceration. Words like power madness, tyranny and Gestapo methods were bandied about. Mathilda Lochem was the most vocal of all."

DeKok grinned grimly.

"Perhaps it'll stir up something. After all, it *has* to come from that group. I don't care if they all look like little lambs and behave as if they were angels . . . one of them killed two people in cold blood." He paused and took the time to unwrap a stick of chewing gum. He placed it in his mouth and chewed thoughtfully for a while. Then he asked: "Any news from the Coroner?"

Vledder shook his head.

"No. It was Dr. Koning. I wonder if that man ever sleeps," digressed Vledder. "You know, he's been involved with almost every case since you and I started to work together. There's more than one Coroner on the City payroll, isn't there?"

"Oh, yes," said DeKok, "there are at least four, or five, that make 'house calls,' so to speak. I don't know how they divide the assignments, but I'm always glad to see Dr. Koning."

"Me too."

"Well, *did* he say anything?"

"What? Oh, no, as I said. He wondered if there were going to be more . . . since it seemed an exact copy of the last one."

DeKok nodded, chewing contently.

"There are two differences . . . a different victim and . . . Harry Donkers."

Vledder slapped his forehead.

"But we have to set him free, now," he exclaimed. "At once. I'd almost forgotten all about him. How stupid. We *must* phone the Commissaris. In view of the new circumstances, there's no reason to hold him any longer. He was downstairs in his cell when the second murder happened. You could hardly ask for a better alibi. And because of the other similarities, I think it clears him of the first murder."

DeKok stood up, disposed of his chewing gum.

"But *is* he innocent?"

Vledder was amazed.

"You're a fine one to ask that question," he protested. "You were the one who didn't want to arrest him in the first place. You've been against his arrest all along."

"But that's the rub, you see," said DeKok. "First of all I was against the arrest because I don't like for other people to interfere with my cases . . . even a Commissaris, or a Judge-Advocate. Secondly, I felt the arrest happened at the wrong time and on extremely nebulous evidence." He sighed deeply. "From the beginning I never doubted that Harry Donkers did not *physically* kill Black Julie, but . . . that doesn't mean he's innocent."

Vledder laughed without humor.

"That's just splitting hairs. Either he's guilty, or he's *not* guilty."

DeKok looked at him evenly.

"Is it really that simple"

Vledder waved both arms in the air.

"Both murders are copies of each other. That's clear. There is virtually *no* difference. Whoever killed Black Julie, also killed Jennifer Jordan. How, in the name of common sense, could Harry be guilty of killing Jennifer Jordan, his aunt . . . the woman he depended on, financially. Remember . . . Harry Donkers was in his cell, downstairs."

DeKok made a helpless gesture.

"Maybe there's a Last Will and Testament."

Vledder nodded emphatically.

"Of course there is a last will. I haven't seen it myself, but Christine Vanwal told me that Harry Donkers is named as a beneficiary. He inherits the bulk of Jennifer's fortune. In addition there is apparently a legacy for Christine, for services rendered, or something and also hefty gifts to all the members of the circle."

DeKok's eyebrows suddenly rippled in that uncanny way. For a moment it seemed as if the eyebrows were not part of the body at all, but were just about to fly off to some unknown nesting place among the canals. Vledder watched and even though he was familiar with the phenomenon, for a few seconds he was speechless.

"*All* the members?" asked DeKok.

"Oh, yes. According to Christine, Jennifer had settled that many years ago. She wanted the circle to stay together, even after her death. It was one of the conditions for the legacies."

"Compulsory membership until death do us part."

"Right," nodded Vledder. "You could call it that. Jennifer's motivation, her intention was that since in life she contacted the hereafter, she wanted to be able to contact the here and now after she died. Her own spiritualistic circle, probably led by a new medium, would be an excellent point of contact for her."

DeKok sat down and rummaged in a desk drawer. With a faint smile he recognized a bag of licorice that had been lingering far too long in his opinion and he quickly stuffed his mouth with a handful. Then he looked quizzically at Vledder.

"It's rather obvious," he said slowly, "that Jennifer believed unconditionally in the possibility of being able to maintain contact with her circle." He closed his eyes to combat a sudden tiredness. "Were all the members of that group aware of the contents of the Will?"

"I don't know. I mean . . . I didn't ask. But I presume they all knew. When Christine Vanwal told me about the will, they were all there and none seemed surprised."

DeKok groaned.

""On the surface it also means that *all* of them had a motive."

Vledder's eyes widened with sudden interest.

"You're right!" He sounded enthusiastic. "Of course. Just like you said . . . a conspiracy. Despite the obvious differences, they all seemed united on this subject. All along I had the feeling the ladies were holding something back, hiding something."

DeKok shook his head.

"But it doesn't fit. Doesn't compute as you're wont to say. You see . . . Black Julie didn't leave a will."

Vledder lowered his head in his hands.

"But she was killed, anyhow."

The door of the detective room slammed open and Commissaris Buitendam appeared in the opening. He beckoned DeKok with a crooked finger and then walked on to his own office.

DeKok swallowed the last of his licorice and came to his feet. The Commissaris had left his door open and DeKok walked into the office, hands in his pockets.

"Why don't you ever tell me anything?" roared the Commissaris as soon as DeKok had crossed the threshold.

DeKok cocked his head at his chief.

"I don't know what you mean."

Buitendam slammed his fist on the desk.

"The murder of Jennifer Jordan." He looked at his watch with a demonstrative gesture. "More than two hours ago!"

DeKok shook his head sadly, a pitying look on his face.

"Did Mathilda Lochem tattle tales again?"

Buitendam nodded.

"And, of course, I immediately got a call from the Judge-Advocate. Recriminations and panic." He looked up at DeKok who had remained standing. "Did you release Harry Donkers yet?"

DeKok looked innocent.

"He's *your* arrestee," he said acidly, the tone in marked contrast to the blandness of his face. "Your arrestee . . . not mine. You know what I think about his arrest. But if you think Donkers should now be released, you only have to lift the telephone and give the necessary orders."

Buitendam leaned back in his chair. He rubbed his eyes with a tired gesture. Suddenly DeKok felt sympathy for the man who was so obviously unsuited for his job, who would have been better used in an administrative capacity at Headquarters. Anywhere, in fact, but in the midst of the hurly-burly of Warmoes Street Station, the Dutch Hill Street.

"Let it rest, DeKok," said Buitendam after a long pause. His voice was reconciliatory. "It's no use to discuss it any further. The arrest of Harry Donkers was a mistake. I admit that." He spread wide his hands. "I have no choice but to admit it. In view of subsequent events, I can only say that you were right and I was wrong. I've been misled. The hocus-pocus during the seance . . . it was impressive and believable. Besides . . . not to put too fine a point on it, I felt encouraged and supported by the Judge-Advocate." He turned his swivel chair a few times from left to right. Then he gripped the edge of his desk with both hands. "Dammit, DeKok . . . he seemed such a reasonable suspect."

DeKok nodded agreeably.

"That's the trouble with our job . . . so often things are not what they seem."

* * *

DeKok sat behind his desk, his feet on top of it and a dreamy look in his eyes.

"I think," he said, "that Buitendam isn't going to last much longer."

"How's that?" asked Vledder.

"He didn't chase me from the room and he freely admitted he had been wrong, that Harry's arrest had been a mistake."

Vledder was amazed and it showed in his tone of voice.

"I wondered about that, when I didn't hear any doors slam, or loud voices. You mean it?"

"It's true."

"Where is he now?"

"Gone home. We went down together to release Donkers and tell him he was a free man again. I also gave him my sympathies for the death of his aunt."

"What was his reaction?"

DeKok made a vague gesture.

"A bit strange, actually. Shocked, but not spontaneous. It's hard to express. It almost seemed as if he had more or less expected it . . . as if he had prepared himself for her death." DeKok took a deep breath and moved his feet off the desk. He leaned forward and rested his chin in his hands. "And you know what I thought strangest of all?"

"Well?"

"He didn't even ask *how* it happened."

Vledder hissed between his teeth.

"He already knew?"

Before DeKok could answer, there was a loud tap on the glass inset of the door. It reverberated through the almost empty detective room. The three or four other detectives in the room, ignored the noise. DeKok looked expectantly at the door. He did not have to wait long. It opened and a woman was silhouetted against the light in the corridor. Vledder and DeKok recognized her and Vledder got up and walked toward her. They exchanged a few brief words and then Vledder led the way to DeKok's desk.

DeKok stood up as they approached.

"The later the night, the better the company," he said with a gracious gesture toward the visitor's chair next to his desk.

DeKok watched her as she sat down. She was dark-blonde, about thirty-five years old and dressed in a brown, suede coat, thick wool stockings and sturdy, formless walking shoes.

"My name is DeKok," said DeKok, "with kay-oh-kay. How may I help you?"

"I'm Babette," she said in a seductive voice, "Babette Vanson. The man downstairs said that you were still here and thus . . ."

DeKok nodded.

"We're still here, as you see."

She unbuttoned her coat to reveal an ample bosom hidden by a coarse, knit sweater.

"In our family," she said in that sexy voice, "we're not very familiar with the police. Nobody in our family has ever been in contact with the police, but I didn't feel like I wanted to be locked up by you."

DeKok smiled a winning smile.

"I don't think it's as serious as all that." He glanced at Vledder who was unobtrusively taking notes. "I usually only lock up people who have done something to warrant it," he continued. He leaned closer. "And you . . . you are innocent, isn't that right?"

She nodded ardently.

"Certainly. My conscience is clear. But then . . . I'm new to the circle. I took the place of Martha Cologne, after she died."

DeKok nodded sympathetically.

"And what Agatha wants, Agatha gets."

She smiled shyly.

"You understand perfectly. Agatha is indeed very bossy, there's no other word for it. She's always organizing things, telling people what to do." Babette made a resigned gesture. "I can live with that . . . she's always been that way. But now I'm seriously considering not attending any further seances. The first time I went, Black Julie was killed, the second time they arrested poor Harry and the third time, Jennifer was killed. To tell you the truth, I'm afraid of the next time. Who knows what will happen. Lord knows, I can do without disasters."

DeKok raised a finger in the air.

"If you don't attend the seances, you stand to lose a lot of money."

She nodded seriously.

"Agatha told me. That's why she wanted me to attend in Martha's place. Jennifer must have been very rich. All the ladies in the circle are getting a large sum . . . if they remain members." She paused, looked from DeKok to Vledder and back again. "Is Harry still in jail?"

DeKok shook his head.

"He was set free about an hour ago."

With a dramatic movement she placed a hand over her heart.

"That's a load off my mind. Harry has nothing to do with the murders. Agatha says the same thing. She says that you, the police, are going about it the wrong way. You should pay more attention to Annette Leeuwenhoek. That's a mean woman."

DeKok gave her a searching look.

"Does Agatha know you're here?"

Babette Vanson avoided his eyes.

"She's asleep," she said evenly. "She had a headache and in that case I always fix her a glass of warm milk." She smiled secretively. "I mixed a few sleeping tablets in with the milk."

DeKok looked stern.

"Sleeping tablets?"

"Certainly. I didn't want her to know I was leaving. That's why I'm so late. I had to make sure she was asleep."

DeKok was confused.

"But why so secretive? Aren't you good friends?"

She crossed her legs and pulled down on her skirt.

"I don't want to be involved in anything."

"And you are?"

She did not answer. She lowered her head and worried with a button on her coat. Suddenly she looked up.

"You know where the poison is from?"

"What poison?"

"From the murders."

DeKok narrowed his eyes.

"You know?" he asked, a hint of tension in his voice.

Babette Vanson nodded slowly.

"Yes, I do . . . from the shed in Agatha's garden."

13

DeKok looked at Babette Vanson, perplexed.

"From *Agatha's* shed?"

The woman nodded decisively.

"Agatha didn't want me talk to you about it. She thought it would be annoying. But when we heard that Black Julie was killed with Prussic acid, we immediately took a look. We had that stuff in the garden."

"Who's garden?"

Babette Vanson pointed over her shoulder.

"Agatha and Martha have had a garden for more than thirty years in the *Use and Enjoy* complex. They inherited the garden from their parents. It's a nice piece of ground with a comfortable cottage, well, a shed, actually, but comfortable . . . and a glass house. In the summer we sometimes spend weeks there. You really feel you're in the country."

DeKok nodded his understanding. In the thirties the government had made available large tracts of lands near the big cities. The tracts had been plowed, covered by topsoil and parceled out as garden plots to the residents of the nearby cities, who otherwise would never have the opportunity to see another living thing, except the trees along the canals. Over the years people had built tiny, one-room cottages on the properties and it was not unusual for families to spend their summer vacations there, especially with kids. The breadwinner would continue to commute to and from work and supply the staples as needed. Especially during the lean years of the war, the small garden plots had often meant the difference between life and death for many people. Today these plots were worth their square footage in gold and often were passed on from father to son, or from mother to daughter.

"How did you get the poison?" asked DeKok.

"Through Irene Peters."

"The wife of the biologist?"

Babette sighed.

"Martha wasn't all that fanatic. Me either. I prefer bulbs and annuals. But Agatha grows orchids in her glass house. She's very good at it and has created a number of new varieties. She's won some prizes. Toward the end of last year, the plants suddenly died. All her beautiful orchids . . . dead. Apparently some insects had gotten into the glass house . . . beetles, bugs, flies, lice, I'm not sure. But they killed the plants. Agatha asked Irene what she could do about it."

"And?"

"Irene talked to her husband and one day she brought Agatha a can of Asepta."

"What's that? A brand name?"

"Yes, it's a powder to make hydrocyanic acid gas. That's what it says on the label with a skull on it. You have to be very careful with it and Agatha was . . . very careful. You have to follow the directions exactly. The powder itself is dangerous and it makes hydrocyanic acid gas, or prussic acid gas. One whiff and you're dead."

DeKok buried his face in his hands. Babette's story had set wheels in motion. Feverishly he searched for connections and motives.

"And you had that stuff in the shed, just like that?"

Babette Vanson shook her head.

"Of course, not. It was in a separate cupboard, above the sink. There was more of that sort of stuff for the garden. Agatha had written *Poison* on the door with a red marker."

"Was there a lock on the cupboard."

"Ach, no." she said evasively. "No lock. Whatever for? We never had children in our garden. Just adults."

"Who?"

Babette spread wide her hands.

"A few of Agatha's neighbors ... all members of the circle."

"Including Annette Leeuwenhoek?"

Babette licked dry lips.

"Including Annette Leeuwenhoek," she admitted.

DeKok smiled slyly.

"But I thought Agatha didn't like Annette?"

"That's true. Agatha doesn't like her. But if she came, for instance, in company with Mathilda Lochem, you could hardly send her away."

"And that happened?"

"What?"

"That she came with Mathilda?"

"Yes."

"When was the last time?"

"A few weeks ago, when Martha was still alive."

"And since then the poison has disappeared?"

Babette gave him a helpless look.

"We . . . eh, we don't know that. Maybe it was gone before. We only looked after Julie had already been killed."

"And then it was gone?"

"Yes," said Babette, lowering her head, suppressing a sob. "Then it was gone. You could see from the ring in the dust where it *had* been."

"Not a very good housekeeper, then?"

Babette was suddenly wounded in her housewife's pride.

"No, no. Agatha and Martha and me, too, we're excellent housekeepers. But the inside of a cupboard used for storing dangerous chemicals . . . in a garden shed . . . really, Inspector, there are limits." Then, oblivious to the apparent contradiction, she added: "But we washed the windows every week."

She fell silent, abashed at her sudden outburst. Again she fidgeted with a button on her coat, avoiding DeKok's eyes. After a long interval she looked up.

"Please keep this confidential, Inspector. I mean, you mustn't tell Agatha I told you everything. I promised her to keep silent."

DeKok merely looked at her. She moved uneasily in her chair and blushed under the steady stare.

"And what if," said DeKok suddenly, "if Agatha has meanwhile woken up and finds you gone?"

Babette smiled. She looked suddenly younger and prettier.

"I'll just tell her I went for a walk because I couldn't sleep. She stood up and buttoned her coat. "I do that a lot."

DeKok came to his feet.

"Has there ever been a break-in?"

"In the garden . . . the shed?"

"Yes."

She shook her head.

"Never by us. Once, further down, in another lane."

DeKok nodded and made a slight bow as she prepared to leave. He came around the desk and reached out his hand. With gentle pressure he led her toward the door. Before he let go of her hand he searched her face, sharp, observing. There was a friendly grin on his face when he asked the last question.

"How did Martha die?"

Babette was suddenly furious. With a gesture of disgust she pulled back her hand. Her naive, almost childlike posture disappeared and her lips pulled together into a thin line. Her cheeks became red as she contemplated him with hate and contempt. She brought her face close to his.

"Not by poison," she spat at him.

* * *

The next morning DeKok was early back in the station. His short night had done nothing to revive him and he felt weak and listless, as if the short sleep had drained the last little bit of energy from his large frame. His feet were tired and his knees creaked with every movement. To top it all, it felt as if a thousand tiny devils were using his calves as pincushions for their satanic little tridents. It made him grumpy as well as listless. He knew what that particular pain meant. Whenever a case was going badly, when his investigations seemed to take him further and further away from the solution, his legs hurt. He explained it as "tired feet," but the pain was almost unbearable. It did nothing for his state of mind to know that the pain, as he had been assured over and over again, was purely psychosomatic. It was no less real for all that. He reached his desk and with a sigh of gratitude sank in his chair. Slowly, with considerable effort, he placed his feet on the desk.

Vledder, who was familiar with the symptoms, gave him a concerned look.

"Tired feet?"

DeKok nodded with a painful grimace.

"Last night . . . early this morning, on the way home, I was thinking about it all." His voice was slow and sluggish. "Perhaps we should have thrown caution to the wind and we should have had all the ladies of that circle subjected to a body search."

Vledder shook his head.

"I thought about that after Jennifer was killed, but the Law simply doesn't allow that."

DeKok nodded thoughtfully.

"That's the problem with the Law . . . it protects the citizens from excessive intrusion by the police, but it also hampers us in our investigations. In order to search all of them, I would have had to arrest them first. You know, I toyed with the idea, but I was able to resist the impulse. It certainly would not have been fair to the innocent." He made a helpless gesture. "Perhaps we could have obtained a Search Warrant, but with Judge-Advocate Lochem involved, that would have been problematical." He sighed again. "Anyway, it's a good thing that the Law imposes limits on us. Otherwise we would really be living in a police state. That remark about Gestapo methods hurt, you know that?"

Vledder nodded his head in sympathy.

"I know it did. But it's just words," he soothed. Then, more briskly, the young Inspector added: "But we're stuck with it nevertheless. We *have* to solve this case."

DeKok gave him a wan smile.

"You're right . . . we *have* to. We owe it to our reputation . . . and the victims," he added softly.

Suddenly, with renewed energy, he lifted his feet off the desk, stood up and walked toward the coat rack, beckoning Vledder in passing.

"Where are we going?"

DeKok planted the latest version of his ridiculous little hat on top of his gray hair and grinned mischievously.

"Bussum."

"Whatever for?" asked Vledder.

"That's where Annette Leeuwenhoek lives and last night I discovered that there were just a few questions lurking in the back of my mind."

* * *

Vledder stopped in Jan Toeback Lane in Bussum in front of a stately brownstone with a large bay window and an impressive carved door. In the center of the door, underneath a small, barred window, was a door knocker in the shape of a lion with a ring in its mouth.

The Inspectors emerged from the car and walked toward the house. The house was covered with ivy and presented a somber, secluded face to the street. DeKok looked around as Vledder lifted the brass ring in the lion's mouth and let if fall back on the strike plate underneath. He bonged the ring several times and listened to the hollow sound from inside the house. The heavy mahogany door was a perfect sound board. The noise echoed in their ears.

After a few minutes the small window in the door opened. Behind the protective bars they saw the face of Annette Leeuwenhoek. There was a gleam of recognition in her eyes, mixed with suspicion and surprise. The small window closed again and slowly the big door opened.

She wore a purple blouse with a standing collar over a long, black, cashmere skirt. A medallion was suspended from a gold chain around her thin neck.

DeKok lifted his hat.

"DeKok," he said politely. "And this is . . ."

Annette interrupted him.

"You don't have to introduce yourselves," she said sharply. "My memory is not that short." She gave him a stern look. "I take it you're here in an official capacity?"

DeKok placed his hat over his heart and bowed slightly.

"We are," he said formally. "We came all the way from Amsterdam to visit you."

Annette wrinkled her nose as if she had suddenly noticed a bad smell.

"But you already know how I take my coffee."

DeKok ignored the remark, while making a mental note of her sharp intellect. He put his hat back on and shivered.

"It's a bit chilly for this time of year, don't you find?"

Annette Leeuwenhoek hesitated a moment, then she stepped back and invited them in.

"Come in."

The two cops went by her into a large foyer with oaken beams along the ceiling and finely decorated wainscotting around the walls. Discreet light glowed from an invisible source behind the chair railing.

Annette closed the door carefully and led the way to a large, high room with an impressive flagstone hearth in the center.

DeKok examined the walls and noticed a number of excellent copies of landscapes by John Constable in fine, gilt frames. There were also a number of Breitners behind clear glass. He paused in front of an Amsterdam city-scape and lifted the bottom edge away from the wall.

Annette came to stand next to him.

"You like Breitner?"

DeKok nodded.

"I like his impressionistic views of Amsterdam. Always have . . . very colorful and lifelike. Although," he added, "it has lately come to my attention that he used a lot of photographs to create his paintings."*

"Yes," agreed Annette, "but nevertheless his paintings are always full of life."

"Not," said DeKok, pointing at another wall, "like the lovely, but lifeless landscapes of John Constable."

Annette smiled.

"That's why I placed them on opposite walls, because of the contrast." She glanced at him, a mocking smile on her face. "And I notice that the arrangement has an educative value."

DeKok grimaced. The arrogant behavior of the woman irritated him and he did not care for the way she attempted to talk down to him. He controlled his pique.

"I also very much appreciate the French impressionists," he said evenly.

"Me, too."

The subject of painting seemed to have lost all interest for her. She tossed back her head and walked away from him. She sat down in an easy chair across from Vledder and crossed her legs. She folded her fingers together around her knee. DeKok took a glance around, looking for places where the wallpaper might have been discolored. Then he joined the others around the hearth.

Annette Leeuwenhoek, swiped the long gray hair from in front of her face and looked expectantly at DeKok.

"Are you, too, here to accuse me of killing Jennifer?"

DeKok did not answer. Her direct question had disturbed his train of thought. To win time, he rubbed the bridge of his nose with a little finger.

---

* See: *DeKok and the Brothers of the Easy Death*

"When I accuse you," he said finally, "I will have the evidence to back it up."

"Then you don't have that?"

DeKok shook his head.

"Not yet," he said precisely. "But I wouldn't worry, if I were you. It's not the first time in my career that it took me a long time to gather the necessary evidence."

Annette Leeuwenhoek pressed her lips tighter and gave him an angry look.

"I don't feel like," she said, agitated, "I don't feel at all like playing some sort of cat and mouse game with you. I will tell you one more time in no uncertain terms: I have *not* killed my first husband . . . I did *not* murder my sister-in-law, Jane . . . and I certainly am *not* responsible for the death of Jennifer Jordan."

DeKok leaned closer.

"How often have you visited the garden shed of the sisters Cologne?"

Annette sighed deeply.

"Agatha Cologne is a nasty intriguer. She is devilishly clever. Much more devilish and meaner than my reputation. Believe me, her campaign against me is no more than a clever trick . . . a clever trick to put the spotlight on someone else, away from herself." She shook her head. "I never took the poison from the cupboard."

DeKok feigned surprise.

"How do you know the poison disappeared from the cupboard?"

She shrugged her shoulders carelessly.

"Who knows. Perhaps we have the same informer."

DeKok pursed his lips. His thoughts went to a woman with an ample bosom and a rough, woolen sweater.

"Babette Vanson."

Agatha smirked.

"A fat, dumb motor mouth, if you know what I mean. She talks about everybody and everything. I'm sure she told you it had to remain a secret just between the two of you."

DeKok lowered his head and groaned inwardly. He needed a moment to absorb the imaginary slap in the face.

"Then you will also know," he said, unsure of himself, "that we released Harry Donkers."

Agatha nodded, looking at nothing at all.

"I knew *that* even before Babette called me early this morning."

"How?"

Annette Leeuwenhoek leaned back in her chair, a supercilious smile on her face.

"He was here, last night."

"Harry?"

"Yes, Jennifer's nephew. The man who was arrested because of the unholy meddling of Mathilda Lochem."

DeKok kept his face expressionless.

"Why was he here?"

Annette looked at him, the same nasty smile on her face. She played with the chain of the medallion. She clearly enjoyed being the center of attention.

"To talk to me," she said hoarsely. "Harry had some problems."

"With what?"

"He wasn't all that forthcoming during his stay at Warmoes Street and he worried about that. He was afraid it would be charged to him at a later date. He . . . eh, he concealed things."

"Such as?"

"The matter of the ring."

"What ring?"

Annette rubbed away a stray strand of hair. The smile on her face had disappeared.

"A poison ring."

DeKok started to dislike this woman, who doled out information like precious bits of gold.

"A poison ring?" he asked, outwardly calm.

"Yes," nodded Annette. "A ring with a secret compartment that could be opened by a slight pressure in the right spot. It's an antique, of course, and rare even then . . . very old, gold with red sapphires. It was part of the jewelry collection Jennifer inherited from her husband."

DeKok contained his impatience with difficulty.

"What's the matter with that ring?" He almost barked the words.

Annette licked her lips.

"Harry knew there was such a ring and after Jane died, he went to look for it."

"And?"

"Gone."

DeKok had reached the end of his patience.

"The poison ring?"

"Yes, from Jennifer's jewelry case."

14

They left Jan Toeback Lane behind them. It had started to rain and Vledder turned on the wipers. DeKok looked at them. As usual, the hypnotic movement mesmerized him and he had to fight against an intense desire to sleep.

Hastily he searched his pockets and after a few seconds he was rewarded with a roll of peppermints. He peeled one out and offered the roll to Vledder, who shook his head. Something else was bothering the young man.

"Out with it," said DeKok.

"It wasn't my fault," apologized Vledder. "I interrogated Harry Donkers several times, but he never said anything about a ring. Annette was right . . . Harry was less than forthcoming. I always had a feeling he was hiding something."

DeKok shrugged his shoulders and squirmed deeper into the seat.

"Well, we'll have to interrogate him one more time because of that ring. Perhaps he has an explanation for his . . . eh, his reticence." He smiled. "But I think it's an interesting angle. I have wondered how the poison was administered."

"Are there still rings like that?"

DeKok nodded.

"Of course. You should remember that! There were made very popular by the Borgias, although they have been around longer than that. But don't let it worry you too much, I hadn't thought of a poison ring, either."

Vledder shook his head.

"Yes, of course, I remember they existed. But only in museums, I thought. Anyway, it doesn't help us all that much, does it? Jennifer's jewelry case was never locked, according to Annette, and was in the same room where they held their seances. That means that *any* of them could have 'borrowed' the ring."

DeKok nodded, crunching his peppermint.

"And we also don't know how long the ring has been missing. Just like the poison in Agatha's shed. Only after Julie died did Harry look for the ring. It could have been gone for months."

They drove on in silence, each occupied with his own thoughts. DeKok thought he saw a glimmer of hope, but then shook his head. He had again fallen under the spell of the swishing wipers. He hoisted himself up in his seat and cracked the window a little. Vledder nudged him.

"The murderess must have worn the ring during the seances."

"Yes, and she probably still wore it when we arrived." He glanced at his young partner, who kept his eyes glued to the road. "Can *you* remember which of the ladies wore a ring with red sapphires?"

Vledder shrugged.

"I didn't look for it. Besides all women wear jewelry."

"You see," said DeKok, "you can just never be alert enough. I don't remember either." It sounded bitter. "Perhaps we could have pinpointed the perpetrator right now."

Vledder drove past Old Bridge Alley and parked the car on the dock behind the station. Instead of using the back entrance, they walked around the building to the front.

"When is the autopsy on Jennifer's body?" asked DeKok.

"It's scheduled for three, this afternoon. Dr. Rusteloos will do it himself."

"You'll be there?"

"Of course."

"Don't feel like it, do you?"

"No, but you won't go."

"Oh, well, nasty jobs like that are for the younger people on the force. I've had my share."

They entered the station house. Meindert Post waved a telephone receiver in the air as soon as he saw them.

"Somebody on the phone," he roared in his usual loud voice.

"Really?" asked DeKok, walking toward him. "Lucky thing you're on the other end. The caller can just hang up and still hear you."

"Very funny, DeKok," said Post, handing him the receiver. Before DeKok could acknowledge the call, Meindert handed him a slip of paper. "And you're supposed to call this number," he added, before returning to his own duties.

DeKok looked at the number on the scrap of paper. He did not recognize it. He handed the paper to Vledder. "You call it," he said and spoke into the receiver.

"DeKok here."

"Peter Karstens," he heard.

"Hello, old paint waster," grinned DeKok.

Karstens could not let that pass.

"I'm not even half as old as you are. And if you had been only half as good a detective as I'm a painter, you'd be Chief Constable by now."

DeKok laughed heartily. He knew he would never be promoted beyond his present rank, but it did not bother him in the least. He was happy where he was, doing what he was doing. His seniority and his undoubted expertise guaranteed him full employment until the day he retired.

"What can I do for you?" asked DeKok.

"Ask rather what I can do for you . . . perhaps I can help you."

"With what?"

"I have a surprise for you."

"What kind of surprise?"

"It's right here, barely six feet from where I'm standing. If you come over, I'll show you."

"Can't you just tell me?"

"If you promise to come anyway."

DeKok nodded with his ear to the receiver.

"I'll be there," he promised.

"All right . . . it's a Monet."

DeKok swallowed.

"What!?"

DeKok stared at the receiver. The painter had hung up. Pensively DeKok replaced the receiver on Meindert's phone. Then he beckoned Vledder who was using another phone across the room. Five minutes later they were back in the car.

* * *

Vledder took his eyes off the road and looked a question at DeKok.

"Where to?"

"North Market."

"What's there?"

"Who's there."

"All right, all right . . . *who's* there?"

"A forger," grinned DeKok.

"A forger?"

DeKok nodded happily.

"It's about time you meet him. As a well-rounded Inspector, you should know people like that." Then he changed the subject. "Whom did you call?"

Vledder grimaced.

"Christine Vanwal."

"What did she want?"

"She wants us to circulate a missing person report."

"Who's missing?"

"Harry Donkers. Babette Vanson told her that Harry was released last night."

"And?"

"He did not come home. Because Harry stays away some nights, she thought nothing of it. But when he still hadn't shown up today, she became worried. Especially at this time she needed Harry badly. There was so much to do . . . Jennifer's funeral, discussions with the lawyer . . . about the will."

"Who's the lawyer?"

"Anthony Pool, Esquire . . . from Purmerend."

DeKok pulled his lower lip and let it plop back several times.

"Does she, Christine, I mean, know anything about Viola Weinbaum?"

"No, I don't think so. She never mentioned her. She did say that she had called everywhere, but that Harry had simply vanished."

DeKok looked thoughtfully at the streets as they slipped by. There were a thousand questions in his mind. Why did Harry immediately upon his release visit Annette Leeuwenhoek? Just to tell her that a poison ring had disappeared? And where could he be? He glanced at Vledder.

"As soon as we're back at the station, why don't you give the doorman at Viola's condo another call?"

"What good will that do?"

"Maybe he can tell us when was the last time he saw Harry's Jaguar." He paused. "And let's call that lawyer as well. I'm curious to know how much friend Harry has cost his dear aunt over the years." He suddenly realized where they were. "Here, at the end of North Market make a left turn. Behind the Reformed Church is where we're going."

They stopped in front of the small house with the large window. DeKok hoisted himself out of the car and waited impatiently for Vledder to lock it. Karstens was waiting for them by the door.

"I was waiting for you," the painter said smugly. "I knew you'd come at once."

DeKok pointed at Vledder.

"My colleague, Inspector Vledder." He grimaced. "Almost as good a cop as I."

Peter Karstens shook hands with Vledder.

"That's supposed to be a compliment?" he asked with a sneer.

DeKok acted as if he had not heard. He placed a hand on the shoulder of the painter.

"And this," he said formally, "is Peter Karstens. If he had lived three hundred years ago, his famous canvasses would be hanging in the best museums in Europe . . . in the world."

Karstens shrugged impatiently.

"Who knows," he said with a grin, "what they will be hanging three hundred years from now."

They walked into the show room.

"Where is it?" asked DeKok.

"The Monet?"

"Of course. Don't be coy."

"Downstairs. What do you think?" There was genuine amazement in his voice. "Use your head. You think I put it here . . . where every passer-by can look at it. If I did that, the place would be empty by morning." He led the way down the stairs to the living quarters. The settee was empty. DeKok missed her at once.

"Where's Maria?" he asked.

At that moment a door opened and Maria entered from what was obviously a bathroom. A cloud of steam, followed her. She was dressed in a towel, wrapped around her hair. Vledder and DeKok gaped. DeKok stammered a greeting. Vledder's mouth was wide open, unable to make a sound.

She stopped when she saw the two men and turned, giving them a full view of her gorgeous body, unobscured by so much as a single strand of hair from her head. She placed her hands on her hips and assumed a challenging pose.

"Good morning," she said calmly. Then she cocked her head slightly at the two Inspectors and added: "Tweedle Dee and Tweedle Dum?"

Before any of them could react, she turned on her heels and walked into a bedroom across from the bathroom.

"She does that," remarked Karstens casually. "She hates clothes and takes any opportunity to show off her body." He paused. "But, of course, it's magnificent, don't you agree?"

DeKok agreed at once and Vledder merely nodded, still dumbfounded.

Karstens walked over to an easel and placed his hand on the cloth that covered it. The bedroom door opened again.

Maria emerged, dressed in a black skirt, a demure white blouse and sensible shoes. Her still damp hair had been pulled up in a pony tail. Vledder stared again. He realized that in the short time she could not have had time to put on underwear. The thought excited him. She brushed her lips against Peter's cheek, nodded pleasantly at the two cops and disappeared up the stairs.

"Where's she going?" asked DeKok.

"To work. She works for a temp service. She types beautiful letters for a respectable office." He grinned. "For the wine. When the supply runs down . . . Maria goes to work."

DeKok shook his head.

"I thought you made millions?"

Peter spread wide his arms in a helpless gesture.

"An honest piece of bread . . . a bit of cheese . . . a glass of wine . . . what else can you buy for millions?"

Without further ado he removed the cloth from the easel.

"Voila . . . Monet."

DeKok stood as if nailed to the ground. He absorbed the glorious painting in silent admiration . . . the loose, easy way of painting, the joyous use of colors . . . the near careless brush strokes . . . he was transported. Slowly, shyly, he came closer. He bit his lower lip from deep appreciation.

"A real one," he panted.

Peter Karstens nodded devoutly.

"A real Monet," he said. "So real that I could have painted it myself."

DeKok looked scared.

"You didn't, did you?"

Karstens shook his head.

"No, no," he soothed, "I didn't make this one. This is a real, original Monet." He smiled thinly. "Thankfully I'm still able to recognize my own work."

DeKok leaned closer and with the tips of his fingers he carefully stroked the slight bumps and valleys in the paint. He looked up at Peter.

"Is it for sale?"

Karstens nodded easily.

"For any reasonable price. I have it, you might say, on consignment."

DeKok straightened out.

"On consignment?"

"Sure. If you happen to know a qualified buyer . . . keep me in mind."

DeKok looked at the artist.

"Where?" he asked, tension in his voice.

"What do you mean?"

"Don't play games, Peter, where did you get it? Who has given you this painting on consignment?"

Karstens looked him straight in the eyes.

"Annette Leeuwenhoek. Dropped it off less than an hour ago."

15

For several seconds DeKok stared at the artist. He did not seem very surprised.

"Annette Leeuwenhoek?"

"Yes," answered the painter. "Annette Leeuwenhoek. She owns this fine Monet, Apparently there's also a certificate of authenticity, but she didn't bring that. Forgot. But as soon as I have a buyer, she said, she'd bring the certificate."

"You have the address?"

"Sure, Bussum, Jan Toeback Lane."

"Why is she selling it?"

Karstens shrugged.

"Maybe she needs money ... who knows. She was a bit nervous when she left the painting ... not nearly as sharp and assured as when she ordered the copies. To me she seemed to be under a lot of tension."

"Did she say anything about that?"

Peter Karstens shook his head.

"Not a word. She was in a hurry when she came and she was in just as much of a hurry when she left."

DeKok rubbed his chin.

"Did you sign a receipt for the canvass?"

Karstens grimaced.

"Not even that. Of course, she can always claim ownership through the certificate of authenticity. Besides, I'm not about to cheat her. It's enough if I can make a commission on the sale. I happen to know a few people who might be interested." He grinned broadly. "If you weren't such an impoverished civil servant . . . I'd sell it to you."

DeKok laughed gaily at the thought. Then his face became serious.

"I *do* want to borrow it."

Karstens was taken aback.

"Borrow?"

DeKok nodded as if he borrowed priceless paintings everyday.

"For about an hour . . . I'll bring it right back."

Peter Karstens laughed half-heartedly.

"A Monet," he said incredulously. "I don't even know if it's insured . . . and if so . . . for how much."

DeKok seemed unconcerned.

"It doesn't matter. I'll guarantee you'll get it back undamaged."

Karstens snorted.

"What's the value of a guarantee like that?"

DeKok gave him a winning smile.

"Our friendship," he said simply.

Karstens rubbed the back of his neck. He was obviously torn between several decisions.

"All right," he said after a while. "But if you're not back in an hour, *with* the painting, I'll go to Warmoes Street and file a report for theft and I'll insist they'll put out a circular, or whatever you call it, for location, apprehension and arrest of the famous art thief . . . DeKok."

DeKok laughed, relieved.

"Nice, Peter, very apt. I'll personally make sure that the Arrest Warrant is issued."

The artist took him by the arm. His face was serious as he pointed at the Monet.

"All kidding aside, DeKok. That is an expensive piece of paint. Irreplaceable. I wouldn't know what to do if . . ."

DeKok raised his hand. He was as serious as the painter.

"I know it's valuable, Peter. It has already cost two lives."

* * *

They drove away from North Market. The Monet was safely stowed on the back seat, carefully wrapped in clean linen.

"It's already past three. You better go directly to the autopsy. You can't keep Dr. Rusteloos waiting."

"And what about you?"

"I'll take the car."

Vledder took his foot off the gas and slowed down. He gaped at DeKok.

"You?" he asked, hastily bringing the car back up to speed and redirecting his attention to the road.

"Yes," said DeKok.

"You are going to *drive*? With that expensive painting in the back?"

"Don't worry about me. I'll use the siren, if necessary."

"All right, on your head be it."

Vledder knew that DeKok was the worst driver in all of Holland and DeKok would be the first to agree.

"Relax," said DeKok. "*Needs must when the devil drives*."

"You could have chosen a less ominous homily," growled Vledder. Then, curiosity getting the better of him: "What are you going to do with the painting?"

"I'm going to show it to somebody."

"Who?"

DeKok remained silent. His thoughts were running ahead of his mind. Why did Annette want to sell the painting so suddenly? Was she under pressure? And if so, who, or what was exerting that pressure . . . Harry Donkers?

"Who are you going to show the painting to?" asked Vledder impatiently.

DeKok stared out of the window.

"Christine Vanwal," he said wanly. "I have seen the same Monet in Jennifer's house."

* * *

DeKok's face was red and he sweated profusely as he manoeuvered the recalcitrant VW through the busy traffic. The grinding of the gears competed with the loud noise of the engine whenever he depressed the gas pedal and clutch pedal at the same time. He despised driving. Engines were a mystery to him and he considered transmissions as something invented to make engines more unmanageable. He also could not understand the behavior of the other drivers on the road. They passed him on the left and on the right. They never did that to Vledder. It all tended to make him more nervous and restless than he was already. He longed for a horse-drawn carriage, or better yet, a quiet canal boat, pulled by a well-trained horse.

He managed to park without hitting any other cars, or winding up in the canal. Thankfully the stately elms were protected by steel posts and therefore only the VW's fender suffered.

Carefully, he took the canvas from the back seat and crossed the quay to the house. The door was immediately opened as soon as he rang the bell. Panting, with the sweat still on his back and in his palms, DeKok climbed the stairs.

Christine Vanwal was waiting for him in almost the same spot where Harry Donkers and Agatha Cologne had awaited him on earlier occasions. Her black, graying hair rested loosely on her shoulders. She seemed surprised to see him.

"Do you have news about Harry?"

DeKok placed the painting carefully on the floor.

"No, no news about Harry. We still don't know where he is." He smiled a friendly smile. "But I'm sure he can take care of himself."

Christine folded her hands.

"But I still worry about Harry. Harry isn't the kind of man to be alone . . . he can't stand it. Whenever Jennifer and I were gone for a few days, he . . ."

DeKok interrupted her.

"I'm not here because of Harry."

She looked suspicious.

"Not because of Harry?"

DeKok shook his head. He picked up the painting and walked down the corridor toward the room at the end. Behind him he heard nervous footsteps. At the end of the corridor he opened the door to the room where the seances were held. With the wrapped painting in one hand he stopped and demonstratively studied the walls. There were two Renoirs, a Monet and a Toulouse-Lautrec. None of the paintings were missing.

He pulled a chair away from the table and placed the painting on it. Carefully he removed the wrappings and after a few seconds the painting was revealed in all its glory.

DeKok kept an eye on Christine. He looked at her face and saw her pale. Her lips quivered. With a smile on his face he pointed at the paintings on the wall.

"I see," he said jovially, "that they are still here. Good." He licked his lips with a nervous gesture, feigning embarrassment. "You . . . eh, you see," he stammered, "I . . . eh, I was afraid one of them was missing." He pointed at the painting on the chair. "I just happened to see this at an art dealer, this morning, and I thought I remembered seeing a similar painting in this room. You know . . . on an impulse . . . I, eh, I came to the conclusion that it had been stolen from this house. So I went into the store and confiscated the work." He spread his hands in apology. "Obviously I was mistaken." He pointed at the painting on the chair. "This must be a copy."

Christine Vanwal nodded almost imperceptibly.

"Indeed," she said tonelessly, "it must be a copy."

DeKok rewrapped the Monet and took it under his arm. He looked up and laughed sheepishly.

"Sorry to bother you," he said. He shrugged his shoulders. "That's what happens when amateurs get involved with real art."

DeKok walked toward the door. Just before leaving the room he stopped and turned around. She stood next to the chair he had used for the painting. Straight as an arrow, the arms folded over her breast.

DeKok looked at her. For an instant he seemed indecisive. Then he turned and walked down the corridor.

* * *

"Anything new at the autopsy?

Vledder grimaced.

"I thought Dr. Rusteloos was being paid for piece work."

DeKok laughed heartily.

"He was in a hurry, was he?"

Vledder nodded.

"It's very fascinating to watch him work under pressure. The man is so knowledgeable, so experienced, that you tend to forget what he's doing. Terrible, really. But he was finished in less than an hour and a quarter."

"And?"

"Nothing particular. It's almost certain that Jennifer was killed by a poison, the same as Black Julie. I asked the doctor if there were any differences between the two cases and he gave it as his considered opinion that there were none. If Black Julie and Jennifer Jordan had not ingested poison, it's likely they both would have lived healthy and long lives."

DeKok censured him with a look.

"Rather cynical, Dick."

Vledder made a helpless gesture.

"Well, if you're not a cynic when you start this job, you'll be one by the time you're no longer a rookie."

"No, no, no," objected DeKok. "That's the wrong way to think. There are too many cops already like that. Just because we frequently come in contact with the seamier sides of society, doesn't mean the whole world is rotten. It's the easy way out. It's like the so–called student riots in the sixties and seventies. The papers, radio, television, they were full of it. Nobody ever mentioned the thousands, hundreds of thousands of students that attended classes regularly and eventually graduated to become decent and productive members of society. Yet all students were blamed. For a while the word student was synonymous with hooligan."

"All right," conceded Vledder, "maybe I'm tired."

"Of course, you are. Just don't lose your perspective."

Vledder sat down behind his desk, automatically powering up his computer. The gesture had become as natural to him as pulling up a chair was to the average person.

"What about the doorman at the condo?" asked DeKok.

Vledder grinned suddenly.

"I think Viola Weinbaum must be pining away. Harry hasn't been around for several days."

DeKok looked interested.

"But Viola is home?"

Vledder nodded.

"Sure. The doorman talked to her only this morning, when she picked up her mail in the lobby. Nothing special, they talked about the weather. He didn't notice anything peculiar." He paused. "But I have a surprise for you."

"What sort of surprise?" asked DeKok.

"That's hard to say. I also called the lawyer, Pool. Christine had already delivered all the papers."

"And?"

"Harry never got a dime."

"Nothing?" DeKok was surprised.

Vledder shook his head.

"The lawyer told me that Jennifer only lived off the interest of her capital. She never touched the principal. As a matter of fact, she never used all the interest either, so the principal grew and grew."

"Interest?" asked DeKok.

"Right, about thirty thousand a year."

"That's all?"

"Yes. Of course, there was no mortgage on the house, but that thirty thousand paid for the housekeeping."

DeKok swallowed.

"Took care of Jennifer, Christine and Harry?"

Vledder nodded.

"You see . . . with that sort of budget there was no room for extra funds for Harry. Certainly not enough for expensive cars and condos in Purmerend."

DeKok rubbed the bridge of his nose with a little finger. Then he stuck the finger into the air.

"Harry had other sources of income," he declared pontifically.

Vledder snorted.

"That's obvious. But we don't know what they are. It's too bad we only just found out, otherwise we could have grilled him about it."

DeKok nodded slowly.

"And his continued disappearance is starting to intrigue me. It seems best if . . ."

The telephone rang. Vledder picked it up and started to take notes as he listened. Suddenly his face fell.

DeKok beckoned with his head. Vledder placed a hand over the mouthpiece.

"Annette Leeuwenhoek," hissed the young Inspector. "She's been murdered."

16

After a while Inspector Vledder replaced the receiver and stared into the distance. He was white around the nose and had a pinched look to his face. The news had obviously shocked him.

DeKok came from behind his desk and placed an encouraging hand on his partner's shoulder.

"Murdered you said?"

Vledder nodded, still dumbfounded.

"At home, in Bussum."

"How?"

Vledder looked pained.

"Crushed skull."

DeKok absorbed that in silence.

"Murder weapon?"

"A heavy poker from the fireplace."

"Signs of a break in?"

Vledder shook his head, regaining his composure under the routine questioning.

"Annette Leeuwenhoek must have allowed her murderer to come into the house." He paused. "Therefore she must have known him, or her. An acquaintance, in other words. We saw ourselves how careful she was about opening the door."

"Anything else?"

Vledder looked at his notes, his busy fingers on the keyboard. Despite the shock he had transferred almost all of the hastily written information into his computer.

"She was roughly in the middle of the room, prone, with severe trauma to the back of the head. A heavy poker with traces of blood and hair was next to her on the carpet."

DeKok pursed his lips.

"Multiple blows," he said.

"Right. The Bussum police suspect that Annette turned her back on her killer and then was attacked."

"So, the murder weapon was already on the premises. It wasn't carried in."

"Yes, does it make a difference?"

"Maybe not."

"Any sign of a struggle, or a quarrel."

Vledder looked vague.

"No obvious signs. The neighbors didn't hear anything, either. One of them, who was walking his dog, thought it strange that the front door was open and that the light was on in the foyer. He called the police."

"While the killer fled in panic?"

"It seems that way."

"What time did it happen?"

Vledder shrugged.

"They weren't sure. One of the neighbors, on her left, said that she had talked with her around nine o'clock that night. They happened to be in the backyard at the same time. Annette told her about our visit that morning in connection with the murders in Amsterdam. That's why Bussum called us at once."

"The name of the neighbor?"

"Mrs. Julia Gruyter."

"So she told the Bussum police and the Bussum police, thinking there might be a connection, called us?"

"That's about it. Is there a connection?"

DeKok looked pensive.

"She was married, wasn't she?"

Vledder looked bitter.

"She didn't get along with her second husband, either. They'd been living apart for some time and that's why she used her maiden name. But the Bussum police has already informed the husband. According to the Inspector who called, they had to be careful. There had been a lot of friction between the couple and they didn't rule him out as a possible suspect. But apparently he had an airtight alibi."

DeKok pulled his chin.

"It's probably best," he said, "if you go to Bussum and take a look around. You can then explain our part of the situation at the same time."

Vledder hesitated.

"I didn't tell you the most important part."

DeKok looked at him sharply.

"And that is?"

"They saw a strange car in Jan Toeback Lane . . . a car that had never been there before."

"I can guess," said DeKok.

"Yes," said Vledder, "a red Jaguar."

* * *

DeKok paced up and down the large detective room, avoiding obstacles without paying attention. The latest developments had shaken him. Just when he thought he was near a solution, somebody changed the game. He had not expected this latest incident and it proved that the opposition thought he was close as well. Things were happening too fast . . . almost too fast to get a grip on them. He *had* to prevent further victims. Victims of a dark game that, he was convinced, had started during a seance in an old canal house.

He stopped in front of Vledder's desk.

"Don't tell the police in Bussum anything about the red Jaguar." He shook his head. "I don't think they'll know it's Harry's car. And I want to talk to Harry before they nail him in Bussum."

Vledder looked confused.

"How are you going to talk to him . . . he has disappeared."

DeKok nodded to himself.

"Who is the best shadower we have in this station?"

Vledder didn't hesitate for a second.

"Graaf . . . Jan Graaf."

"The Giant of Warmoes Street," smiled DeKok.

"What?"

"That's what the underworld calls him, because of his large physique. But he *does* know how to follow someone without being noticed. He has proved that many times. He has his own methods." DeKok thought for a moment. "And also Gerrit Lindt."

Vledder looked doubtful.

"Is that a responsible combination? The only thing those two have in common is that they both have a beard."

"Doesn't matter," said DeKok, squashing all further objections. "Get hold of them."

"Who do you want shadowed?"

DeKok raised his index finger into the air.

"Viola Weinbaum," he declared as if that was obvious.

* * *

"Anything new from your visit to Bussum?"

Vledder shook his head.

"The police were busy . . . a lot of people. Their technical people found fingerprints on the scene of the crime."

"Where?"

"Especially on the poker."

"Very nice. Have they been able to identify them yet?"

"Not as far as I know. They were busy with it, though."

DeKok gave him a calculating look.

"You fingerprinted Harry Donkers when he was staying here, didn't you?"

"Sure, part of the normal routine."

DeKok merely stared at him until Vledder suddenly slapped his forehead.

"If the Bussum police send the prints here, for identification, we've got Harry right away."

DeKok shrugged carelessly.

"But that would be hardly a surprise, now would it? I'm sure there's a logical explanation for Harry's fingerprints in Annette's house."

Vledder did not agree.

"Even if there are prints on the murder weapon?"

At that moment Aad Ishoven, chief of administration, interrupted by placing a copy of an invoice in front of DeKok.

"I won't pay this," exclaimed the administrator excitedly. "It'll be the thin end of the wedge. Petty cash was never meant for *this*."

DeKok gave him an annoyed look.

"What sort of invoice is this, anyway?"

"From Graaf," snorted Ishoven. "Seventy five guilders from a flower shop in Purmerend . . . for roses."

"Roses?"

Ishoven spluttered with indignation.

"He said it was on orders from you."

DeKok picked up the invoice and stuffed it in his breast pocket. His fingers fished around for a few more seconds and he pulled his hand back with a piece of hard candy between his fingers.

"I'll look into it," he promised the administrator, starting to unwrap the candy.

Vledder leaned closer.

"The fingerprints on the poker," he insisted.

DeKok's phone rang. With an irritated gesture Vledder picked up the receiver.

"Detectives," he barked into the harmless instrument.

DeKok watched and listened intently, trying to follow the course of the conversation.

"What is it?" he asked finally, softly.

Vledder covered the mouthpiece.

"They found Harry's hiding place."

"Where?"

"An old farm, less than five miles from Purmerend."

"Who's on the other end of the line?"

"Graaf."

DeKok smiled.

"Tell him you're coming."

Vledder finished the conversation and replaced the phone.

"Why do I have to go to Purmerend?"

DeKok had a simple answer for that.

"Assist in the arrest of Harry Donkers."

"On suspicion of murder?"

DeKok pursed his lips.

"No," he said carefully, "not murder. Blackmail."

It was Vledder's turn to look thoughtful.

"Blackmail?" he repeated, unsure he had heard right.

"Got it in one," praised DeKok. "And ask Graaf what's up with the roses."

Vledder shook his head, bemused.

"And you?"

DeKok stood up and went to the coat rack.

"I'm going to visit Mathilda Lochem."

"But why?"

DeKok grinned, a mischievous twinkle in his eye.

"I'm going to ask her to arrange another seance."

* * *

DeKok gazed slowly around the room. The low, intimate room with the heavy beams along the ceiling, the large oaken table with high-backed chairs in the center and the cheerful impressionist paintings on the wall had become familiar to him. It was the fourth time he had visited the room and he fervently hoped it would be the last time.

On his left was Peter Karstens. He seemed out of place, dressed in a black silk shirt, green velvet trousers and suede boots. DeKok had had some difficulty in convincing the artist to help him with the investigation. "I don't want anything to do with your capitalistic world," Karstens had said indifferently. He had changed his opinion when DeKok had asked him pointedly how he would react if the victim had been his own, lovely Maria. DeKok regretted having had to use such insensitive tactics, but he had no other choice. He needed the painter for the evidence he intended to gather.

To his right was Vledder. The dissatisfied look that had marred the young man's face all morning, had disappeared. DeKok had informed him of his plans and in Vledder's eyes he saw the same tension that filled him.

There was a faint smile on the face of the gray sleuth. In the kitchen, on the long counter, waited the coffee cups. Despite heavy protests, he had insisted that the tradition of coffee before the seance, was to remain intact. Vledder had made the coffee and cleared away afterward, to make sure the cups would not again disappear in soapy water. That would not happen this time, because in the kitchen were Bram Weelen, experienced police photographer . . . and Kruger, the old dactyloscopist.

The women were near the three narrow windows, nervously and anxiously, huddled in small groups. Their whispered voices stilled when DeKok raised an arm with a theatrical gesture.

"I do offer you all my apologies," he said. "I've misled you." He pointed to his left. "This man is *not* a spiritualistic medium, as I introduced him. His name is Peter Karstens, an artist, a painter of some renown, who is a master of virtually all painting techniques and can readily copy any style from modern, as well as old masters." He pointed at the walls. "Many of these unique works, he has assured me, are by his hand." DeKok paused. He looked at each of them individually, but could detect no reaction to his words. "Therefore," he continued, "there will be *no* seance here today. I have gathered you here in memory of the passing of Black Julie, Jennifer Jordan and Annette Leeuwenhoek . . . three women from your circle, who died a violent death."

DeKok glanced briefly aside. Vledder had not taken his eyes off the women. DeKok added a last sentence.

"The woman who killed all three, is among you . . . and I know who she is."

There was an immediate murmur of voices. The women looked at each other with shock and suspicion. Then they again formed a close, silent front against the intruders. Agatha Cologne stepped forward, fire in her eyes.

"If you know who she is," she challenged him, "why don't you arrest her?"

DeKok looked at her intently.

"I want you to point her out yourselves."

Agatha Cologne was overwhelmed.

"Us? We?"

DeKok nodded. With a casual gesture of his hand he relegated her back to her place among the women.

"Men," he said in a didactic tone of voice, "usually pay little attention to jewelry worn by other men, or by women. They also tend to wear less jewelry than women. I realize that's a generalization, but it's nevertheless true. Perhaps men are less vain, perhaps men display their vanity in other ways, I won't get into that. But my *experience* has taught me that women usually know exactly what sort of jewelry is worn by other women."

DeKok paused, studied the women with that frank, insulting stare of a cop.

"The poison," he went on, "with which Julie and Jennifer were killed, was hidden in a ring . . . a poison ring . . . a unique piece, very old and very valuable ... decorated with red sapphires. The murderess wore that ring when she killed."

For a moment the women looked at him in utter confusion. Their mouths gaped and it was easy to follow their thoughts from the various expressions that fled across their faces as they considered the implication of his words. Then, slowly, almost imperceptibly, there was a movement among them. Slowly they moved away from each other. Only one of them did not move . . . did not move until she stood alone in the middle of a rough circle of women. She was very pale and her lips quivered. She wore a plain suit of a simple cut. It looked vaguely like a Salvation Army uniform. Slowly DeKok approached her and placed an official hand on her shoulder.

"Christine Vanwal," he said formally, "I arrest you for murder . . . multiple murders."

17

The doorbell rang.

DeKok and his wife walked toward their front door together and DeKok opened it. Outside was Jan Graaf. He was immaculately dressed in a dark, blue suit with a pearly gray necktie. There was a friendly grin between beard and moustache.

"Come in," invited DeKok heartily.

Graaf brought his right hand from behind his back and offered a big bouquet of red roses to Mrs. DeKok.

Mrs. DeKok blushed.

"They're gorgeous," she said with admiration and cradling them in her arm, she took the flowers to the kitchen.

Graaf gave DeKok a wink.

"Those were left over."

"From what?"

Graaf made a nonchalant gesture.

"From the seventy five guilders I thought I'd spend on roses."

"I meant to ask you about that."

Graaf grinned wickedly.

"That shadowing is dumb work, you know." It sounded contemptuous. "And Viola Weinbaum is one good looking girl . . . a picture . . . everything on it and with it. So I thought: I'm not going to follow her, I'll court her. With a bunch of flowers in my hot little hands, I rang her doorbell and had my little say . . . that I was in love and all that. Well, after that she didn't think it at all strange when she saw me sitting in my car in front of her building." He grinned again. "Yesterday afternoon she came out and rushed to her car. Obviously she was in a hurry. I stepped out of my car and addressed her."

"With roses?"

Graaf smirked.

"Of course, again with roses. She told me she had no time for me right then and drove off. Gerrit Lindt followed her and I followed Gerrit. Easy as pie."

"Until you got to the farm."

Jan Graaf nodded.

"I told you, easy as pie."

DeKok patted the large cop on the shoulder and led the way to the living room, where the others had gathered.

DeKok had invited Vledder, Jan Graaf and Gerrit Lindt for an informal gathering at his home. He liked to do that after a case had been solved. Over the years it had become a tradition that many cops looked forward to.

DeKok lifted a large bottle of cognac and showed the label. That was followed with grunts of anticipated pleasure. While he poured the precious liquid in the waiting snifters, Mrs. DeKok came in with large tray of delicacies, especially prepared to accompany the drinks. A cozy fire smoldered in the fireplace to drive away the slight chill of the cool summer evening.

DeKok lifted his glass.

"To crime," he proposed.

Mrs. DeKok gave him a censorious look.

"One doesn't toast crime," she said.

DeKok feigned amazement.

"But without crime there would be no detectives."

Graaf and Lindt laughed, but not Vledder. He stared somberly into the distance, apparently oblivious to those around him. Although he had been involved from the very beginning with the murders in the canal house, he did not see all the connections and it bothered him. After Mrs. DeKok had changed the toast to "To us," and they had taken their first sip, Vledder leaned forward, burning eyes on DeKok's face.

"Graaf, Lindt and myself," he started, "arrested Harry Donkers yesterday in an old farm. The reason for the arrest, according to you, was blackmail. Who was the victim of his blackmail?"

DeKok took another appreciative sip of his cognac before he leaned back in his chair. He waited for the soft, smooth liquid to reach his stomach and then he placed his glass on a small table next to him. He smiled at Vledder.

"The evil genius in this entire affair," he said, "was Annette Leeuwenhoek. Every single criminal idea was born in that sickly mind. There are still rumors that she poisoned her first husband and it's now unimportant how much truth there is in those rumors. By now Annette will have been judged by Him, who knows all facts . . . even without the police."

He paused and nodded to himself. His hand went back to his glass. He lifted it and cradled it between his cupped hands, warming the liquid inside.

"I've come to the conclusion that at the root of almost every criminal act is a moment of lovelessness, in other words, the *absence* of love, or the *denying* of love. I'm beginning to believe that more and more. This moment of lovelessness came about when Jennifer Jordan refused to lend Christine Vanwal the money to buy an apartment in a building for the elderly. They call that a service flat, I believe."

"Service flat?" asked Vledder, obviously wondering what DeKok was talking about.

"Yes," explained DeKok, "a building with individual apartments, where groceries and other shopping is delivered to the door and where a doctor and nursing staff are on twenty-four hour call. No stairs, but ramps or elevators, railings in all the corridors . . . surely you know what I mean?"

"Yes, of course," said Vledder. "For old people, who do not want to go in a rest home, but want to remain independent. But I mean, what does that have to do with Christine Vanwal. She wasn't nearly old enough, nor, I think, was she an invalid."

"You're right, unless she was an invalid of the mind. But all right," he said hastily, upon catching a glance from his wife. "About four years ago," he explained, "Christine's father died. Because of a daring . . . perhaps unwise policy, his business had suffered a number of losses, substantial losses. In order to save the business from bankruptcy, he had taken a heavy mortgage on his house. After his death, his wife was unable to carry the mortgage. She asked for help from her daughter."

DeKok took another sip, but hastily continued his story when he saw his wife making a movement as if to take away his glass.

"Christine Vanwal wanted to make sure that her mother was taken care of for the rest of her life. She thought a service flat was the ideal solution. After all, the old lady was still spry enough not to need constant care, or even the extra care provided by a rest home. But Christine had no money of her own. She never received any salary for her work in Jennifer's house. Therefore, it was sort of logical that she would ask rich Jennifer for a loan."

Mrs. DeKok looked up.

"Jennifer refused?"

"Yes," sighed DeKok. "And that was the beginning of all the misery. At one point Christine discussed her worries about her mother with Annette Leeuwenhoek and she also told her that

Jennifer had been unwilling to lend her the money. Annette had an immediate solution."

Vledder could not contain himself.

"What sort of solution?"

DeKok grinned at his impatience.

"The reasoning was simple . . . what does a blind woman want with beautiful paintings . . . if she can't see them? Annette Leeuwenhoek, who knew quite a bit about paintings, had often before looked at the paintings in Jennifer's house with envy and avarice. She told Christine that the paintings were worth a lot of money and she also said that she knew somebody who could forge the originals in such a way you wouldn't be able to tell the difference . . . especially not if you were blind."

Vledder saw the light.

"Peter Karstens," he said with a beatific smile.

DeKok smiled, having no trouble reading the expression on Vledder's face. The young man was at that moment more occupied with the memory of Maria then with that of the painter.

"How's Celine?" asked DeKok suddenly, referring to Vledder's fiancee, who was a flight attendant for KLM, Royal Dutch Airlines.

Vledder was suddenly flustered.

"Still on intercontinental routes," he said, avoiding DeKok's eyes.

Mrs. DeKok who did not miss much came to the young Inspector's rescue.

"Don't tease, my dear," she said. "Go on with your story."

"As soon as I have had a refill," pouted DeKok.

Graaf hastened to hand him the bottle and after DeKok had poured himself a generous measure, Graaf refilled the other glasses.

DeKok continued as if there had been no interruption.

"Exactly," he said, "our friend Peter. Annette gave him the commission to make copies of two Renoirs and a Monet. When Jennifer, accompanied by Harry, was attending a concert in the Concert Gebouw, the paintings were exchanged."

"Clever," grunted Lindt.

"Yes, indeed. But Annette, who was to sell the *real* paintings, cheated immediately. She sold the Renoirs, but kept the Monet. And from the money she made out of the Renoirs, she held back a large sum. The remainder was divided between her and Christine. But even the diminished amount was sufficient to buy a service flat for Christine's mother and that's all she really wanted."

Gerrit Lindt interrupted again.

"But didn't the nephew, Harry, discover that the paintings had been changed when he came home?"

DeKok shook his head.

"Nobody noticed. When the ladies of the circle gathered for their next seance, nobody remarked upon it either." DeKok grinned. "I tell you ... Peter Karstens is a remarkable craftsman."

Vledder waved impatiently, his drink forgotten in his hand.

"When did Harry Donkers become part of it all?"

"It was again Annette Leeuwenhoek who engineered that, albeit against her will. Apart from paintings, Jennifer also owned a valuable stamp collection."

"Lowee talked about that," knew Vledder.

DeKok made a selection from one of the platters that had reached him and chewed thoughtfully on a croquette. He swallowed.

"Annette used the same reasoning as with the paintings ... what use is a valuable stamp collection to a blind woman ... when she cannot see it? She exchanged the valuable stamps for worthless ones of the same size and shape."

Mrs. DeKok shook her head in wonderment.

"What wickedness."

"You're right," agreed DeKok, "even Little Lowee and his underworld pals thought it beneath them to steal from a blind person." He suddenly imitated Lowee's gutter language to perfection. "*You don't steal from no blind person, you just don't,*" he said, quoting the small barkeeper.

They fell silent for a moment. Then Vledder urged again.

"Go on," said the young man.

"Well, yes, as I said, they started to exchange the stamps. But that was the first real mistake they made." He placed his empty glass on the little table. "Harry Donkers knew nothing about paintings, but . . . he knew all about stamps. Before long he noticed that the more valuable specimens had disappeared from the collection so he called Christine Vanwal to account. After he threatened her with telling everything to his aunt, Christine confessed everything . . . also about the paintings."

Vledder looked relieved.

"The blackmail," he exclaimed. "Finally we're getting there. Our Harry had found a little gold mine."

"Exactly," answered DeKok. "Nephew Harry who was kept on a short leash by his aunt and who was always short of cash, blackmailed Christine and Annette."

Vledder laughed.

"And from the money he bought an expensive car and Viola's little condo in Purmerend."

"It takes a thief to catch a thief," observed DeKok. "There was not a single cloud in their criminal sky and they could have continued their practices without worry if . . . Jennifer hadn't found a doctor who promised he could restore her sight."

Jan Graaf pulled on his beard.

"Panic in thiefland," he paraphrased.

"You're right. Fortunately, or unfortunately, rather . . . it was again Annette Leeuwenhoek who had the solution . . . Jennifer Jordan must not have her sight restored."

Mrs. DeKok moved to the edge of her chair.

"What a snake," she said.

DeKok looked serious.

"At that moment the basis for the murders was agreed upon, the necessity accepted. Annette proposed poison. Possibly because she had used it with success in the past. Christine hesitated. At first she shrank back from the very idea of murder. But Annette was very persuasive and eventually Christine agreed.She even agreed to do the actual deed, provided . . . it was a fast acting poison, so that Jennifer's suffering would be minimized as much as possible."

Gerrit Lindt had a question.

"What about Harry Donkers?"

DeKok waved a hand in the air.

"In his defense I can say that Harry Donkers knew nothing about the murder plans of the two ladies. They kept him in the dark . . . possibly because he was also marked for elimination."

"To be killed?" asked Mrs. DeKok. She swallowed, knowing the answer.

"Yes," said her husband. "The devilish duo had come to the conclusion that they had paid blackmail long enough."

Vledder frowned.

"But now I'm confused all over again. Why did they kill Black Julie?"

DeKok lowered his head.

"The murder of Julie bothered me no end," he said in a tired voice. "I have to confess that I didn't understand it at all. No matter what I tried . . . I simply could not find an acceptable motive. It seemed so senseless. Finally I thought . . . is there a motive at all? Perhaps Black Julie died by accident. Perhaps she was not the target of the murder attempt. There could have been a mistake. And if there *was* a mistake . . . how could it have happened?" He paused, a painful look in his eyes. "Then I started to ask the ladies how they took their coffee and it soon became evident that Julie and Jennifer not only sat next to each other at the table, they also drank their coffee the same way . . . lots of milk and sugar."

Mrs. DeKok tapped him on the knee.

"You better explain that. What does it mean that they both drank their coffee the same way?"

DeKok briefly covered her hand with an affectionate squeeze.

"It means that the *content* of the two cups looked exactly the same . . . that *those* two cups could have been exchanged. If somebody drinks her coffee black, or with just a hint of cream, they won't reach for a cup that is obviously loaded with milk and sugar. You take another cup. But when the contents between two cups looks exactly alike . . ." He stared in the distance, as if recalling the scene. "In any case, it's certain that the cups were exchanged. Why Julie took Jennifer's cup will always remain a mystery. Maybe her own cup, the cup in front of her, wasn't exactly clean . . . maybe a trace of lipstick had remained on the cup. Maybe Jennifer's cup was a little fuller. Remember, by being late, Julie had missed her first cup of coffee. Whatever the reason . . . unwittingly Black Julie chose death."

"Wow," said Lindt.

"Yes, wow, indeed. Christine Vanwal confessed this morning and she told me about her shocked surprise when she saw Julie lift Jennifer's cup . . . the coffee with the poison. She said she wanted to get up . . . to scream . . . but she was so paralyzed by fear that she could only watch, horrified, while Black Julie died before her eyes." DeKok pressed his lips together, a bitter expression on his face. "Quick and painless . . . as had been planned."

"But by thinking of a mistake," said Vledder, surprised, "didn't you at once conclude that the murder of Julie was instead aimed at Jennifer."

DeKok shook his head sadly.

"I *should* have understood that at once, but there was not a shred of evidence for my theory. Just a suspicion . . . that was all. Also, I still did not know from where the danger was to be expected. When Jennifer Jordan died a few days later, I felt betrayed and depressed. I had an overpowering feeling of failure. And I was angry . . . angry with myself for my impotency, my inability to catch the perpetrators. Marie Vaart was closer than she knew when she accused me at the time of just making a speech to confess how powerless I was."

"But . . ." said Graaf. DeKok held up a hand. Graaf fell silent.

"But," continued DeKok, "at that moment I *did* get an idea that eventually led to the solution. Mathilda Lochem had told me that Jennifer was to be operated on next month by Professor Hemming and that she most likely would again be able to see. The question, therefore changed . . . it was no longer *why would anyone kill a blind woman?* but rather . . . *why would anyone kill a woman who would soon see again?* And the answer was obvious: Because she would see things she wasn't supposed to see."

"The paintings," said Vledder, who had a habit of stating the obvious at times.

DeKok nodded and in response to a silent hint, received the bottle from his wife. He poured another measure in his glass and then took a quick sip.

"My throat was getting dry," he said. "Well, the rest is quickly explained. I had seen the paintings in Jennifer's house and I knew they were good. I mean . . . as fakes they were excellent. And there was only one man who was able to produce such perfect work . . . Peter Karstens. So I followed a hunch and had a delightful visit . . ." He paused and looked at his wife who smiled indulgently. "As I said a delightful visit in Peter's studio and he told me that Annette Leeuwenhoek had ordered a number of copies, two Renoirs and a Monet." he smiled. "There was finally some light at the end of the tunnel."

Graaf leaned closer.

"What did Annette say about it?"

DeKok shook his head.

"I didn't tell her. I merely hinted, during our visit to her, that I was interested in French Impressionists. Maybe I scared her, because almost immediately after our visit she contacted Peter Karstens and brought him the Monet she had kept behind. Obviously she had no idea that I had already spoken with him."

"Sneaky," said Graaf.

"Perhaps. I borrowed the Monet from Karstens and used a silly excuse to show it to Christine. Christine must have realized at that time that the game was up. She also realized that Annette had cheated her. She finally came to the conclusion that Annette was responsible for her getting into the trouble she was in. She decided to do away with Annette. She figured she had no chance of using poison on Annette . . . Annette was too smart for that and also forewarned, so to speak. Christine took more drastic measures."

"The poker," said Vledder.

DeKok rubbed the bridge of his nose with a little finger.

"Kruger and Weelen compared the fingerprints on the coffee cups with the photos of those found on the poker. Christine's prints were a perfect match."

For a while everybody concentrated on eating and drinking, each occupied with their own thoughts. Then Graaf broke the silence.

"So, as I understand it, Harry Donkers has nothing to do with any of the murders."

DeKok smiled to himself, glad to see that Vledder was not the only one to state the obvious.

"No, he's not even an accessory. But he *did* suspect, as soon as Julie died, who was responsible. That's why he went looking for the ring. His arrest was actually convenient for him . . . no matter how strange that may sound. He considered it protective custody, because he felt he could be next. That also explains why he wasn't really surprised when he heard his aunt had died. He knew he was dealing with a couple of extremely dangerous women."

"I don't blame him for hiding," said Mrs. DeKok.

"Me either," said her husband. "After his release he first went to see Annette to make sure they knew he had seen through them. He also made sure she understood he was not about to become the next victim."

Vledder cocked his head at DeKok.

"But why would Annette tell us about the missing poison ring?"

DeKok made a helpless gesture.

"I'm not sure . . . and we can't ask her anymore . . . but I think it was a last desperate attempt to push off all the guilt on Christine, blame her for everything. After all, Christine was the woman who actually administered the poison."

There was another silence. Mrs. DeKok disappeared in the kitchen to make coffee. Soon she returned with a tray. Lindt hastily offered his help and DeKok poured another round. Vledder passed around a plate with assorted cheese. The conversation became more general. The horrible murders in the spooky canal house were relegated into the background.

Vledder leaned back in his chair. He stayed aloof from the general conversation. Something seemed to worry him. Suddenly he sat up straight and addressed DeKok.

"During the second seance," he said, "while the Commissaris and the Judge-Advocate were present, the board pointed to Harry as the perpetrator. Christine later explained why that was in error. I thought her explanation was reasonable ... acceptable." He paused and raised a finger in the air in a subconscious imitation of one of DeKok's gestures. Mrs. DeKok smiled secretively. "But," continued Vledder, "during the first seance, the board spelled out 'Jane dies.' And, you see, *that* bothers me. At that moment nobody in the circle could possibly know that Jane Truffle, alias Black Julie, was about to die. You see ... it was impossible for anyone to arrange that. The announcement regarding Jane's death *must* have come from the hereafter."

DeKok swallowed. His face was serious when he spoke.

"There are more things in heaven and earth, Dick Vledder, then are dreamt of in your philosophy."

"That sounds familiar," answered Vledder, "you just made that up?"

"No," said Mrs. DeKok, "it's Shakespeare ... Hamlet, act one, scene five ... near the end," she added sweetly.

Everyone was surprised, except DeKok who grinned proudly.

About the Author:

Albert Cornelis Baantjer (BAANTJER) first appeared on the American literary scene in September, 1992 with "DeKok and Murder on the Menu". He was a member of the Amsterdam Municipal Police force for more than 38 years and for more than 25 years he worked Homicide out of the ancient police station at 48 Warmoes Street, on the edge of Amsterdam's Red Light District. The average tenure of an officer in "the busiest police station of Europe" is about five years. Baantjer stayed until his retirement.

His appeal in the United States has been instantaneous and praise for his work has been universal. "If there could be another Maigret-like police detective, he might well be Detective-Inspector DeKok of the Amsterdam police," according to *Bruce Cassiday* of the International Association of Crime Writers. "It's easy to understand the appeal of Amsterdam police detective DeKok," writes *Charles Solomon* of the Los Angeles Times. Baantjer has been described as "a Dutch Conan Doyle" (Publishers Weekly) and has been called "a new major voice in crime fiction in America" (*Ray B. Browne*, CLUES: A Journal of Detection).

Perhaps part of the appeal is because much of Baantjer's fiction is based on real-life (or death) situations encountered during his long police career. He writes with the authority of an expert and with the compassion of a person who has seen too much suffering. He's been there.

The critics and the public have been quick to appreciate the charm and the allure of Baantjer's work. Seven "DeKok's" have been used by the (Dutch) Reader's Digest in their series of condensed books (called "Best Books" in Holland). In his native Holland, with a population of less than 15 million people, Baantjer has sold more than 5 million books and according to the Netherlands Library Information Service, a Baantjer/DeKok is checked out of a library more than 700,000 times per year.

A sampling of American reviews suggests that Baantjer may become as popular in English as he is already in Dutch.

ALSO FROM INTERCONTINENTAL PUBLISHING:

TENERIFE! (ISBN 1-881164-51-9 / $7.95) by Elsinck: A swiftly paced, hard-hitting story. Not for the squeamish. But nevertheless, a compelling read, written in the short take technique of a hard-sell TV commercial with whole scenes viewed in one- and two-second shots, and no pauses to catch the breath (***Bruce Cassiday*, International Association of Crime Writers**); A fascinating work combining suspense and the study of a troubled mind to tell a story that compels the reader to continue reading (***Mac Rutherford*, Lucky Books**); This first effort by Elsinck gives testimony to the popularity of his subsequent books. This contemporary thriller pulls no punches. A nail-biter, full of European suspense (**The Book Reader**).*

MURDER BY FAX (ISBN 1-881164-52-7 / $7.95) by Elsinck: Elsinck has created a technical tour-de-force. This high-tech version of the epistolary novel succeeds as the faxed messages quickly prove capable of providing plot, clues and characterization (**Publishers Weekly**); This novel by Dutch author Elsinck is so interestingly written it might be read for its creative style alone. It is sharp and concise and one easily becomes involved enough to read it in one sitting. MURDER BY FAX cannot help but have its American readers fall under the spell of this highly original author (***Paulette Kozick*, West Coast Review of Books**); This clever and breezy thriller is a fun exercise. Elsinck's spirit of inventiveness keeps you guessing up to the satisfying end (***Timothy Hunter*, [Cleveland] Plain Dealer**); The use of modern technology is nothing new, but Dutch writer Elsinck takes it one step further (***Peter Handel*, San Francisco Chronicle**).

CONFESSION OF A HIRED KILLER (ISBN 1-881164-53-5 / $8.95) by Elsinck: Elsinck saves a nice surprise, despite its wild farrago of murder and assorted intrigue (**Kirkus Reviews**); Reading Elsinck is like peeling an onion. Once you have pulled away one layer, you'll find an even more intriguing scenario. (***Paulette Kozick*, Rapport**) Elsinck remains a valuable asset to the thriller genre. He is original, writes in a lively style and researches his material with painstaking care (***de Volkskrant*, Amsterdam**).

* Contains graphic descriptions of explicit sex and violence.

Also From InterContinental Publishing:

VENGEANCE: Prelude to Saddam's War

by Bob Mendes

Shocking revelations concerning his past move Michel Moreels, a Belgian industrial agent and consultant, to go to work for the Israeli Mossad. His assignment is to infiltrate a clandestine arms project designed to transform Iraq into a major international military power. Together with his girlfriend, Anna Steiner, he travels to Baghdad and succeeds in winning the trust of Colonel Saddiq Qazzaz, an officer of the *Mukhabarat*, the dreaded Iraqi Secret Police. At the risk of his own life and that of Anna, he penetrates the network of the illegal international arms trade, traditionally based in Brussels and the French-speaking part of Belgium. He meets American scientist Gerald Bull, a ballistic expert. Gradually it becomes clear to Michel that neither Bull, nor Anna, are what they appear to be. The more he learns about international secret services and the people who are determined to manipulate him, the more his Iraqi mission takes on a personal character: one of Vengeance!

A "faction-thriller" based on actual events in Iraq and Western Europe.
A Bertelsmann (Europe) Book Club Selection.
First American edition of this European Best-Seller.

ISBN 1-881164-71-3 **($9.95)**

Bob Mendes is the winner of the (1993) "Gouden Strop" (Golden Noose). The "Golden Noose" is an annual award given to the best thriller or crime/spy novel published in the Dutch language. "An intelligent and convincing intrigue in fast tempo; in writing *Vengeance*, Bob Mendes has produced a thriller of international allure." **(From the Jury's report for the Golden Noose, 1993)** . . . Compelling and well-documented—Believable—a tremendously exciting thriller—a powerful visual ability—compelling, tension–filled and extremely well written—rivetting action and finely detailed characters—smooth transition from fact to fiction and back again . . . (**a sampling of Dutch and Flemish reviews**).

DEADLY DREAMS
by Gerald A. Schiller

It was happening again . . . the mist . . . struggling to find her way. Then . . . the images . . . grotesque, distorted figures under plastic sheeting, and white-coated, masked figures moving toward her . . .

When Denise Burton's recurring nightmares suddenly begin to take shape in reality, she is forced to begin a search . . . a search to discover the truth behind these horrific dreams.

The search will lead her into a series of dangerous encounters . . . in a desert ghost-town, within the restricted laboratories of Marikem, the chemical company where she works, with a brutal drug dealer and with a lover who is not what he seems.

A riveting thriller.

ISBN 1-881164-81-0
$9.95

A thriller of fear and retaliation, ***Gary Phillips,*** **author of Perdition, USA**; . . . promising gambits . . a *Twilight Zone* appetizer, **Kirkus Reviews**; . . . a brisk, dialogue-driven story of nasty goings-on and cover-ups in the labs of a giant chemical works with a perky, attractive, imperiled heroine, ***Charles Champlin*** **[Los Angeles Times]**.